Matt

Warriors and Wagon Trains During the Civil War

James Pasley
5/14/2019

This book is dedicated to my best friend, my wife Karen.

APRIL 27, 1864
Boone County, 10 miles North of Fulton, Missouri

Josiah patiently sat atop his horse, accompanied by seven other riders, as the Union patrol approached from the valley below. He and his small group were all decked out in Union uniforms they recently acquired after raiding a Yankee wagon train headed to Sedalia. Josiah turned to look at their leader, Bill Anderson. He had been riding with Bill since February 1864, when Bill, along with several other guerrillas, decided to split from their captain, William Clark Quantrill, and head back to Missouri after having spent the winter in Sherman, Texas.

Looking out over the valley below, Josiah still found the beauty of Missouri fascinating. All the trees were budding, spreading a carpet of green over the landscape as far as the eye could see. The flowering dogwoods, with their white blossoms, were sprinkled throughout the forests, and buzzards circled in the clear blue skies overhead, signaling the official start of the spring season.

As he waited for the Union patrol to approach, Josiah thought back to his early days when he rode with Captain Quantrill.

William Clark Quantrill was the oldest of 12 children. He wasn't a Southerner; he was born in Canal Dover, Ohio, on July 31, 1837, to Henry and Carolyn Clark Quantrill. His father was a high school teacher, and at age 16, Bill became a teacher as well and taught in Ohio, Illinois, and Indiana. In 1857, he moved to Miami County in eastern Kansas to try his newfound career of farming. He was 19 years old, and he didn't look like a guerrilla. Bill was a soft-spoken man, standing 5' 9" with reddish-brown hair.

When Quantrill arrived in Kansas, he quickly realized that farming was not what he wanted to do for a living. In the summer of 1859, he took a job teaching school at Osawatomie, Kansas. Due to all the troubles between Missouri and Kansas, the school closed in 1860, and Quantrill roamed the border with Indians and common thugs who made a living by gambling and stealing. Some of the men he ran with were Lawrence, Kansas, abolitionists.

In the winter of 1860, Quantrill was accused of stealing a horse, and fearing the law, he sought a way to escape Kansas. Quantrill joined up with a party of five young Lawrence abolitionists who planned to conduct a slave-stealing raid in Jackson County, Missouri.

Armed with pistols, the men set out for the home of Missouri farmer Morgan Walker, a wealthy planter who owned 26 slaves. When they reached Blue Springs, Missouri, Quantrill told the others that he would ride ahead and scout out the area. What he did instead was ride straight to the Walker farm to warn Mr. Walker's son what was about to happen.

Walker gathered his neighbors and set up an ambush for the Kansas abolitionists. Quantrill rode back to join the Kansans and told them the coast was clear. He and the abolitionists rode to the farm and dismounted. Quantrill knocked on the door and was let into the house as was previously arranged.

Once Quantrill was out of the line of fire, the Missourians cut loose and killed all the free-soilers. The fight at the Walker farm was reported in the Kansas City newspapers, and Quantrill became a hero to the people of Missouri. He went from being a wanted man in one state to a hero in another.

Of course, the newspapers wanted to know who this man was, so he made up a story. He told them he was a native of Maryland who came to

Kansas to join his brother on a trip to Pike's Peak. He said that on the way, he and his brother were attacked by anti-slavery northerners known as Jayhawks, his brother was killed, and he was wounded and left to die along the side of the road. Quantrill allowed how an old Indian found him and nursed him back to health. Having recovered from his wounds, he came back to Lawrence and joined the Jayhawks under an assumed name to seek revenge. Quantrill claimed that the five Kansas abolitionists who rode with him to the Walker farm were the same men who killed his brother.

Bill joined up with several other Missourians and formed his band of guerrillas who all swore to protect the citizens of Missouri from the evildoers in Kansas.

Josiah heard the horses approaching and returned his focus to the present. It was a tough decision indeed to leave Captain Quantrill, but when the Younger brothers, along with Frank and Jesse James, decided to ride with Bill Anderson, and when Quantrill hesitated to return to Missouri that spring, Josiah felt as if he had no choice.

Bill was a strange man, but he would fight. Back in Missouri, he was known as "Bloody Bill." He was a tall man with long, black, curly hair that fell to his broad shoulders. His eyes were cobalt blue. At this point, there was little doubt that, at times, he was insane. The previous fall, what few of his family members remained died in the collapse of a makeshift Union prison in Kansas City where they were being held by the Union military commander, General Thomas Ewing.

From that point forward, Bill vowed to kill every Union soldier he came upon and to wreak havoc on all Missouri citizens who chose to support the Union. Bill loved to see his name in print and recently wrote a letter to the editor of the Lexington newspaper stating, "I have chosen guerrilla warfare to revenge myself for wrongs that I could not honorably revenge otherwise. I lived in Kansas when this war started. Because I would not fight the people of Missouri, my native state, the Yankees sought my life but failed to get me. They revenged themselves by murdering my father, destroying all my property, and since that time, murdering my sisters."

As the Union patrol approached, Bill turned to the men and instructed them, "Stay calm boys, they can't tell us from any other Union patrol. Wait for my signal."

The patrol consisted of nine men led, by their lieutenant. They had no idea the patrol they were approaching was the toughest guerrilla band in Missouri, disguised in Union uniforms. The lieutenant greeted Bill, "Good day, sir; what unit are you with?"

Bill winked at Josiah, and immediately, he and the rest of the boys drew their pistols and opened fire. The Union patrol never stood a chance. All 10 men fell from their horses. A few of the wounded tried to scramble away, only to be chased down and shot. Unbelievably, one of the Union soldiers was still alive. Seventeen-year-old Archie Clement jumped down from his horse, walked up to the man, and casually slit his throat.

Archie was something of a homicidal maniac. He rode with Bloody Bill from the first day and became one of the most notorious guerrillas in Missouri. Not only did he take pride in killing Union soldiers, but he also spread terror throughout the countryside by mutilating the bodies of those he killed. He loved to scalp his victims, and in some cases, beheaded them, leaving them leaning against a tree, holding their own heads.

Josiah and the rest of the boys were horrified of Archie. Thankfully, Bill kept a tight rein on him. Archie would take orders only from Bill, even when Captain Quantrill was running the show. He was so despicable that, during winter camp with the regular Confederate Army, the soldiers would post guards at night for fear that Archie would sneak into their camp and kill even them.

Having picked over the bodies of the Union soldiers for valuables, weapons, and military correspondence, the guerrillas rounded up their horses, mounted up, and rode off in the direction of the Logan farm in Audrain County.

Littleby, Missouri, Audrain County, Logan Family Farm

There was a small knock at the door. Martha Estelle Logan, (known to everyone as Matt) knew it was her father coming to retrieve her. The previous night, she and her parents, along with her brother William and her three sisters, Elizabeth, Georgianna, and Anna, sat at the dinner table where her father told them what they all knew was coming.

"Matt," he said, "your maw and I love you very much, but your relationship with Josiah and the rest of those boys has brought danger to our entire household. Just yesterday, the Union Provost Marshal raided the Johnson place, looking for Bloody Bill and Josiah. They pulled old man Johnson out of bed, dragged him across the front porch, and hanged him from a tree in front of the house, right before his wife and daughter. After that, they took everything of value and burned the house and barn to the ground. They left that woman and her daughter with nothing, and ever since General Fremont down in Jeff City declared martial law throughout the state, there is not a damned thing anyone can do about it. He paused for a moment then added, "Matt, we know you will never stop seeing Josiah, but we also know it is only a matter of time before the Provost Marshall comes for us if you stay here."

Matt knew that leaving was the only option. She loved her family and could not bear the thought of the atrocities her father described happening to her own kin. "Papa," she asked, "where can I go? I am a simple schoolteacher, and I have no money. Anywhere within the state, they will find me."

Her father, known throughout the community as "Uncle Jimmy," answered, "Believe me, your mother and I have thought the same thing. However, we have an answer. Your aunt Sarah and uncle Will are leaving for California on the day after tomorrow by wagon train. Everyone knows your uncle is a Rebel at heart, and he is in a bad situation. So, he is planning to take your aunt and your cousin Lizzie to Sacramento. He also has agreed to take you along."

She made a sour facial expression, so her father declared, "Matt, there can be no discussion, and you know that. Perhaps this terrible war will come to an end soon, and you will be able to return home. You will be in good hands with your aunt and uncle, and Lizzie will be a good companion for you along the trail to California."

Later that night, Matt's mother came to her room. Both women cried ever since the decision was made. Matt's mother was of strong Scottish stock and carried her 5'3" frame well. Most men would describe her as handsome rather than beautiful, but something about her caused all the men to turn their heads in her direction when they saw her.

Her mother pulled a small leather-bound book from her apron pocket and handed it to her daughter. Matt opened the book only to find all the pages were blank. Her mother stated, "This is a gift for you from me and your father. It is a diary." When Matt furrowed her brow but didn't say anything, Mrs. Logan continued, "Matt, these are truly sorrowful times, but you must be strong. Think of this as an adventure, and be faithful in recording the events of your journey each day. You come from a family of strong adventurers. Remember, your grandfather was Hugh Logan, one of the original pioneers of Missouri, and his father was General Logan, who came from the wilds of Kentucky with Daniel Boone. General Logan could have settled in Fort Logan, Kentucky, but instead, he chose adventure. As your father has told you, your grandfather and his dad moved to Missouri from Kentucky with a rifle in one hand and an ax in the other."

Late that night, Matt was awakened when she heard the hinges on the barn door squeak. Someone was in the barn! Matt grabbed the oil lamp next to her bed and tiptoed down the back stairs to the kitchen, where she left the lamp, and then out the back door to the barn lot. As she approached the barn, she could see a faint light and movement inside. Creeping toward the door, a strong hand grabbed her shoulder and spun her around. She let out a yell that she was sure everyone in the house heard. There, standing before her, was Josiah.

Immediately, Matt threw her arms around his neck and hugged him. Josiah reprimanded her saying, "You must be crazy sneaking around out here without any way to protect yourself." She smiled and alleged, "The most dangerous man in Audrain County is standing right in front of me, and I can handle him!"

They both laughed, and with that, Bloody Bill, the Younger brothers, the James brothers, and Archie all came out to greet Matt with huge smiles on their faces. Bill walked up to Matt, gave her a big hug, removed his hat, and stated, "Ma'am, this here troublemaker claims he knows you and your family and that you'd be willing to put us up in your barn for the evening."

Matt laughed out loud again and quipped, "I don't know about the troublemaker, but Bill, you're welcome in my home any time."

At that instant, Matt's dad kicked open the back door of the house with a shotgun in his hand. "Matt, who's there? I'm warning you men, if you lay a hand on my daughter, it will be the last thing you do." Matt hollered back to her father, "No need to worry, Paw! It's only Josiah and the boys."

"Well, for goodness sakes, Matt, show some hospitality, and tell them boys to put up their horses, and come on into the kitchen!" Mr. Logan exclaimed. "I'll bet they're starving."

The men did as they were told, and joined Matt, her father, and mother at the kitchen table. As the men ate, Matt's father questioned them for over an hour, getting the latest news on the war effort. Everyone knew he was a Rebel, and this wasn't the first time he helped guerrilla bands traveling through the area by providing them food, supplies, and shelter. The Logan farm was well known in the bushwhacker community and was often used as a rallying point both before and following guerrilla campaigns.

After the men ate, they headed back to the barn. Matt's folks retired upstairs, leaving Josiah and Matt alone to talk. Matt informed Josiah about her father's plan to send her to California. She told him she wanted to stay and wondered if she could ride along with the boys instead. "I can ride as good as you, you know I can shoot, and I'm a lot better cook than Bloody Bill!"

Josiah smiled and replied, "I can't argue with any of that, but there are two huge problems. First, your father is right. I have talked to several people in town, and they all know about you and me. If they know, the Provost Marshal knows or will soon, and he is an evil man. He will not hesitate to come to this farm, kill your father and brother, burn the place to the ground, and send you, your mother, and your sisters off to the Gratiot Street Prison in St. Louis. You and I cannot let that happen. For that reason, you must do as your father says and head to California until this all blows over. I promise, when the time is right, I will come for you."

Matt, with tears in her eyes, inquired, "You said there were two huge problems; what is the other one?" Josiah stood, walked to the kitchen door, turned, and confessed, ... "I love you." Then, he put on his hat and headed into the dark night for the barn.

Matt sat for the longest time trying to figure another way, but there was simply no choice. In addition to using her family to capture Bloody Bill, she knew the Provost Marshal would use her as bait to hunt down and kill Josiah.

The next morning Matt rose early, dressed quickly, and ran downstairs and out through the kitchen door to the barn. When she got there, she could see that Josiah and the boys were gone. Next to the door was a note.

Dearest Mattie,

I cannot tell you how happy I was to see you and your family last night. A messenger came early this morning and told us that the Provost Marshal is in Huntsville, Bill's hometown, and he is wreaking havoc with the people there. He is using Kansas troops to enforce his raping and pillaging of the town. Duty calls, and we must continue to do our part to protect the citizens of Missouri from a federal government that is entirely out of control.

As we discussed last night, you must go to California. Do this for me and know that I am thinking of you every day and fighting to bring this war to an end so that you and I can be together again. Be strong and show those people along the trail just how tough a Missouri woman is.

Love,

Josiah

Matt folded the note carefully and stuck it in her pocket. She would carry it with her as she headed west.

Huntsville, Randolph County, Missouri

Huntsville was the county seat of Randolph County where Bloody Bill was born and educated. At the age of 14, he moved with his father, his brother Jim, and his three sisters to an area near Council Grove, Kansas. Very quickly, the family was caught up in the border war between Missouri and Kansas. Bill's father, who supported the southern cause, was killed by Kansas troops being led by Senator Jim Lane. This group, made up mostly of common criminals, was known as the Jayhawks and conducted regular raids into Missouri.

When word came to Bill and Jim that their father was killed by the Jayhawks, they immediately sought out and joined the Southern guerrilla band known as Quantrill's Raiders. It was then that they met Captain Quantrill, the James boys, and the Younger brothers. Except for Quantrill, all the boys were under the age of 19, and all were homeless, as they all lost their fathers to the war.

Bill and the boys made camp on the outskirts of town. It was early morning, and most of the people of Huntsville were not yet awake. Bill sent Josiah to scout out the town. Except for the county courthouse, Huntsville was like any other small, rural, Missouri town. It had a Main Street fronted by several mercantile stores, a bank, a hotel, two saloons, a livery stable, and a general store. The bank and the courthouse were the only brick structures in town. In the rain, the road turned into a quagmire. For this reason, a six-foot-wide boardwalk ran down both sides of Main Street.

When Josiah returned to camp, he reported, "There is a company of 15 Union soldiers holed up in the county courthouse on the town square. I saw four men hanging by the neck from a huge oak tree on the town square. I asked a local who they were, and he said they were four prominent Huntsville citizens who were accused of being Southern sympathizers. One of them was the bank president."

Upon hearing this, Bill declared, "That makes my decision easy. Mount up, boys; we are going to rob a bank." The men quickly mounted their horses, checked their weapons, and galloped off in the direction of Main Street. As they swept into town, they stopped long enough to burn six houses and the general store, which were all owned by Union sympathizers, as Bloody Bill pointed out. They rode to the bank, and sure enough, three Union soldiers were guarding the money. Josiah and the men opened fire, immediately killing all three. A young bank clerk was found hiding behind the counter. Josiah pulled his pistol and was about to shoot the man when Bill walked in and shouted, "STOP!"

Bill approached the terrified cashier and asked, "You're the Robinson boy, aren't you?" The boy sputtered, "Yes, I am." Bill exclaimed, "I know your father and mother; both have helped me and my men in the past. How are they?" The youth, still fearful, answered, "They were both killed a week ago when the Provost Marshal sent his troops into town. The next day, the soldiers came to the bank and arrested Mr. Byrne, the bank president, and accused him of being a Southern sympathizer. That's him hanging out there in the town square along with Mr. Platt and his son who ran the livery stable, and Mr. Jones who owned the saloon."

Bill looked at the boy and said, "I'm sorry about your maw and paw. We're here to make things right." Then Bill revealed, "We were gonna rob this bank, but now I'm not so sure." The clerk looked at Bill, "Take the money," the clerk insisted. "The Provost Marshal left a skeleton crew here in town and said he'd be back with reinforcements tomorrow to confiscate all of the bank's assets since the president was a Rebel." With that, the clerk opened the safe, put the money in a sack, and gratefully handed all $45,000 in the vault to Bill.

About that time, shots were fired. Earlier, Bill posted the Younger brothers, Jim and Cole, just outside the courthouse. Someone reported to the soldiers that the general store was on fire. As the soldiers filed out with weapons in hand, Cole and his brother opened fire. Seeing that they were outnumbered and had stirred up a hornets' nest, the brothers made a hasty retreat in the direction of the bank. As they approached, Josiah, Bill, and the James boys provided covering fire for Cole and Jim. After rejoining the group, the Youngers and the rest of the gang mounted up and hightailed it out of town.

Randolph County, 10 miles due west of Moberly, Missouri

Bill and the boys made camp in the woods near a small spring. Having finished a meal of venison and beans, the men spread out their bedrolls around the campfire and settled in for the evening.

Cole Younger sat down next to Josiah and offered him a chew of tobacco. Josiah took the tobacco, thanked him, and invited his camp associate to join him in conversation, "Cole, as long as we've been riding together, you've never told me how you and Jim came to be riding with this group."

"Well," he began, "I watched them Union soldiers steal my father's fortune back in 1861 when the Jayhawks rode onto my family farm near Harrisonville and took everything we had. My paw was always a Union supporter and thought this war was crazy. He had a very successful business raising horses and making carriages. When the Union troops showed up, they took it all and used my paw's horses and wagons to haul off all the things they stole from the people of my town. Having lost everything, a few weeks later Paw decided to sell off the 10 head of cattle that the Jayhawks didn't find up on the north 40. With no horse, he had to walk those cattle to the sale barn in Independence. On the way there, a Union patrol, led by a Captain Walley, rode up and shot my paw dead right there on the road and stole the cattle."

When we found out what happened to him, me and my little brother hunted that man down, set up an ambush, and killed him and his patrol. Everyone knew it was us that did it, so we rode out, found Quantrill, and joined up with the southern cause. A week after we left, the Provost Marshal came looking for us, and since Maw and my sisters wouldn't tell them anything, they burned our home and all the outbuildings to the ground."

Younger continued, "Since Maw and the girls lost everything, they went to Independence to live with my aunt. It's a helluva thing, with me being only 17 and Jim 15, that we find ourselves penniless and fighting for our lives as wanted men by our own federal government."

Pausing in thought for a moment, Cole resumed, "I can tell you that Frank and Jesse have a story similar to mine and so does that young boy Riley Crawford that just joined us. His paw, Jepthah, was dragged from the family home in Blue Springs in the middle of the night by the Jayhawkers and shot. After her husband was killed, Mrs. Crawford brought her son to our camp and asked us to make a soldier out of him and revenge his father's death. Riley there is only 13 years old but hates Union soldiers and the Jayhawkers more than any man in this outfit." Reaching into his saddlebag and pulling out a jug of whiskey, Cole asked, "What's your story, Josiah?"

"Well, I lost my paw back in '58 when he traveled west into the Kansas territory to fight those dirty red legs," Josiah commenced. "I never knew how it happened - just got word he wouldn't be coming home. When the war started in '61 with General Beauregard firing on Fort Sumter, everything changed here. President Lincoln called on the states to supply 75,000 troops, and our Governor, Claiborne Fox Jackson, basically told Lincoln he could stick it and that we wouldn't provide a single man to fight against our Southern brethren. Governor Jackson was quite a character. He was born and raised in Missouri and ran a general store. Eventually, he was elected to the Missouri House of Representatives, and during that time, he married the daughter of a prominent doctor in Fayette, Missouri. Unfortunately, his wife died of a fever a year after they were married. So, he started dating her sister. Sure enough, they eventually got married, and two years later, she died of a fever. Then what did he do? He went back and married the third daughter! Dr. Sappington said, at their wedding, "Don't come back again because you can't have my wife!"

Cole and Josiah both laughed, and Josiah continued, "Jackson ran on a platform that he would keep Missouri in the Union, but when he gave his inaugural address, he said we owed it to our Southern brethren to join with the Confederacy, and he called for troops. I heard about all this from a friend on a neighboring farm, so I packed up, kissed my maw goodbye, and headed off to Jeff City to seek revenge for the death of my father. When I got there, over 11,000 local Missouri boys had arrived, just like me. It was quite a sight. Jefferson City only had 3,000 people, and 11,000 of us guys showed up to fight for the governor. The biggest problem we had was that we didn't have any guns. All I had was an old flintlock shotgun, but a lot of the guys had no weapons at all. Governor Jackson called on the former governor and Mexican-American war hero, Sterling Price, to command our newly formed Missouri State Militia, and the decision was made to raid the federal arsenal in St. Louis that held 60,000 rifles and over 1 million rounds of ammo. Only about 600 of the men had sufficient arms to head to St. Louis, so I was told to stay behind with the rest of the boys and hold the capital."

"In May 1861, 800 of our boys set up camp in North St. Louis, planning to take the arsenal. Back then, St. Louis was being run by a powerful politician by the name of Frank Blair, and he called on the local military commander, Union Captain Nathaniel Lyon, to gather his troops when he heard about our boys camped out north of town. Three thousand Union forces surrounded our 800 Missouri boys and forced them to surrender. They marched them through the streets of St. Louis, heading for the Gratiot Street Prison. It used to be a hospital owned by a doctor who was a Confederate sympathizer, and the Union just took it from him and turned it into a prison. As our boys were marched through the streets of St. Louis, the people saw Missouri boys advanced at bayonet point by Federal troops and realized that state rights no longer existed as our Federal Government was out of control. Missourians started shouting and throwing rocks at the Union soldiers. Captain Lyon, who feared he would lose control of his prisoners, gave the order to fire into the crowd. When the smoke cleared, 15 unarmed St. Louis citizens, including women and children, lay dead. As word spread throughout the state about what happened, many people who sat on the fence decided to side up with the governor and the Confederacy."

Cole remarked, "I remember that. I think the papers called it the 'St. Louis Massacre.'"

Josiah responded, "That's right. When Governor Jackson and Sterling Price heard about the massacre, they decided to travel to St. Louis to talk to Captain Lyon and Frank Blair. They met for four hours at the Planters House Hotel. Governor Jackson said he'd stay in the Union provided all federal troops were removed from the state of Missouri. Frank Blair said that was totally unacceptable, and the meeting turned into a shouting match. Captain Lyon roared, 'If I have to kill every man, woman, and child in the state of Missouri to keep it in the Union, I will do so— this means war!' Then he instructed his second-in-command, 'Escort these men across my lines.' Governor Jackson and Sterling Price were taken to the train station where they boarded and headed back to Jefferson City. On the trip back, they stopped at the Gasconade and Osage River crossings and blew up the bridges, so Union troops would be slowed down in coming to occupy the capital. When the governor and Price arrived in Jeff City, they cleaned out the state treasury of several million dollars in gold, gathered the rest of us guys in the militia, and we headed for Boonville, a town made up of former Tennessee and Kentucky families, where we knew we would be welcome."

Cole took a swig of whiskey and recalled, "I remember hearing about that. Captain Lyon loaded his men on steamboats and showed up in Jeff City with his Union forces several days after you guys left town. He then got with the local German immigrants living there, and they went door-to-door arresting every person the Germans identified as Confederate sympathizers. My uncle lived there at the time and was arrested and taken to the capitol building where they turned the basement into a makeshift prison. As I recall, Captain Lyon took off on his steamboat the next day and headed for Boonville."

Cole passed the jug of whiskey to Josiah who took a swig, wiped his mouth, and responded, "That's right. I was there in Boonville with Governor Jackson and General Price when Captain Lyon and his 1,700-man force came to shore in Boonville. With the small force we had, we didn't stand a chance, and the battle only lasted about 30 minutes before we had to pull up stakes and hightail it out of there. We were outnumbered 5 to 1. As the Union was advancing, I ran up to Governor Jackson's tent and warned him that the enemy was just down the road. From what I understand, Governor Jackson and the two men with him, seeing they had run out of time, stuffed the gold in a cannon barrel and buried it. The governor told them they would come back for it later. That sure didn't work out. Both men were killed since then and Governor Jackson died of consumption in the winter of 1862. To this day, nobody knows for sure where all that gold is buried."

Cole looked at Josiah with wide eyes and asked, "Then what happened?" Josiah continued, "Well, like I said, we were outnumbered 5 to 1, so, we headed south, hoping to make our way to Arkansas where we could get reinforcements from the regular Confederate Army. After all, we were just a bunch of local Missouri farm boys being led by a rogue governor and a former Mexican-American war hero. At that point, we weren't part of an army; we were just a state militia being pursued by Federal troops. As we headed south, we started recruiting as many men as we could, and by the time we reached Springfield, Missouri, we had 5,200 men with us. Captain Lyon, with the force of 1,700, thought he was chasing 300 to 400 of us. We continued to let them think that way and led them straight to a little farm outside Springfield called Wilson's Creek. Word reached St. Louis of Captain Lyon's so-called victory at Boonville, and those fools field promoted him to general. That pompous ass Lyons made the decision to try to sneak up and attack us in the early morning hours of August 10. What he didn't know was we were waiting for him, and in addition to our troops, we met up with Confederate Brigadier General Benjamin McCullough and 2,200 Confederate soldiers. I have to admit, those Union soldiers put up one helluva fight, especially considering we were on the high ground, but eventually they ran out of ammo, were worn out, and retreated to Springfield. It was an ugly affair, and both sides lost over 1,000 men that day. After the battle, as we collected our dead, we found the body of General Lyons. He was the first general from either side to be killed in the war."

"After the Battle of Wilson's Creek," Josiah spoke on, "Governor Jackson and General Price approached Confederate General McCullough and asked if he would join them in a push to retake the capital of Missouri. McCullough told both men that there wasn't a chance in hell he was going to drive his troops into a state that voted for a governor who they thought would keep them in the Union. He said he might just as well lead his forces into Boston. So, he returned to Arkansas with his men as the governor and General Price led our ragtag army back north into central Missouri as an independent military unit at war with the Federal Government and no support from the Confederacy."

"General Price led us north to Lexington, Missouri, on the Missouri River," Josiah continued. "There was a Union fort there commanded by a Yankee colonel, who was an Irishman by the name of Mulligan. General Price knew the guy and had fought alongside him in the Mexican-American War. The fort had over 3,500 soldiers, but our little army grew to nearly 6,000. The trick was how to sneak up on the fort. General Price asked the men if any of them could play music, and many of them said yes. As we marched to the fort, he put the musicians out front and had them play an Irish jig. Colonel Mulligan heard the music and thought it was a Union force passing through the area who struck up a tune to pay tribute to the colonel. This allowed us to march right up to the fort before we opened fire. Mulligan and his men were stunned and surrendered after a short battle. They had over 200 casualties; we had only 75 and took 3,500 prisoners. Problem was, we didn't know what to do with 3,500 prisoners. So, we helped ourselves to weapons and supplies while the governor and General Price decided our next move. The fort had a telegraph, and the next day, we were able to intercept a report that said General John Fremont was headed to Jefferson City, heard about our capture of Lexington, and was sending 40,000 troops there to capture us. With that information, Governor Jackson and General Price gave the order to mount up and head back to Arkansas. It was at that point, I made the decision to go home. I decided I wanted to fight this war on my own terms and not be led around by a bunch of politicians and former generals. A lot of the guys in our little army made the same decision. The rest of the boys headed back south and joined the regular Confederate Army. I went home for a little while, and when I heard Quantrill was in the area, I sought him out and joined up. Been riding with him ever since. That's my story, Cole."

"I had no idea you were involved in all that. Seems like all of us have a story to tell. We'd better get some rest, Josiah," concluded Cole. "We got a long day in front of us tomorrow."

Railroad Depot, Littleby, Missouri, Audrain County

April 27, 1864 (Diary)

"I am leaving home today for the Golden Land. It is raining and oh so muddy. When will I ever spend another night here surrounded by family and friends? Maybe never. God help me to bear this trial and teach me the way that is right."

These were the first words Matt scribbled in the diary which her mom gave her. She wrote as she sat alone waiting for the train to arrive to take her to St. Joe. She insisted her family not see her off at the train station. It was more than any of them could endure. It also might give any federal collaborators the impression that the pro-Confederate Matt broke off from the rest of the Logan family and was being sent away.

As she waited for the train, memories of the life she was leaving flooded her mind. Matt was born and raised on the family farm of 320 acres in southwest Audrain County. Her grandfather came to Missouri from Fort Logan, Kentucky, before Missouri became a state in 1821. He took a job in Fulton, Missouri, as a carpenter, worked hard, and finally saved enough money to purchase the farm in Littleby. He built the farmhouse where Matt's father was born, and when he passed on, he left it to Matt's father. It truly was a beautiful place. Nestled in the rolling hills along a spring fed creek, half of the property was cleared for pasture, and the other half was left in timber. Pecan trees, shagbark hickories, and majestic oaks dominated the woods, making it seem more like a city park than a wilderness. Matt spent her happy childhood there.

Matt's father planted beans and corn, just as his father did, and also a massive crop of turnips. Mr. Logan learned from an old German the value of planting turnips. Turnips kept well and could be fed to the cattle and hogs throughout the winter. Additionally, in tough times, the family could survive on turnips, and Matt's mother became very creative in different ways to prepare them. Recent times were harsh, and Matt, quite frankly, hoped she would never have to eat another turnip as long as she lived!

Matt excelled in her studies while attending the local one-room schoolhouse.

April 28, 1864 (Diary)

"I took the train this morning and came to St. Joe. Arrived at 3 o'clock this morning. Had a tolerably pleasant trip, pleasant company, rained nearly all the time. Aunt Sarah, Uncle Will, and Cousin Lizzie met me at the Pacific Hotel and have been with them ever since. The wagon train was not ready to leave here for California when I arrived. I do not like the prairie. I like to be where I can see nature and listen to the free wild birds of the woods and inhale the sweet perfume of the flowers in nature's own garden. I am impatient to leave this place, to be traveling

westward."

The Pacific Hotel in St. Joseph, Missouri, was filled with anxious people waiting for their journey to begin. St. Joseph was founded in July 1843. The town expanded rapidly starting in 1849 when the first gold rushers used it as a jumping off point to head West. St. Joe outfitted the prospectors with tools, horses, mules, oxen, wagons, and all the provisions they could ever need. Many set out for the West on wagon trains, averaging about 14 miles a day. Some simply set out on foot. Soon thereafter, steamboats brought thousands of prospectors to St. Joe during the late 1840s and early 1850s.

A short time later, the Hannibal to St. Joe railroad was complete. This line passed directly through Littleby, Matt's hometown. On February 13, 1859, Joseph Rubidoux, the founder of St. Joe, drove the final spike in the line that would connect St. Joe with Alton, Illinois, and then all the way to Chicago.

Immigrants came to St. Joseph by the thousands to join wagon trains headed westward along the Oregon Trail. The travelers, for the most part, lived in tent cities on both sides of the Missouri River while they waited to take wagon trains West. Mattie, her aunt, uncle, and cousin were lucky to have found a room at a hotel.

Matt, worn out from her travels and late arrival, awoke about 9:00 a.m. and found a note from Aunt Elizabeth saying they were on Main Street looking for supplies. Matt looked out the window of her hotel room. The city was alive with people and commerce all due to the wagon trains that streamed through it, waiting to cross the river by ferry where it was only a quarter mile wide. The ferry boats ran night and day hauling wagons across the river to begin their journey west. All day long, people came to the city, and the busy Hannibal/St. Joseph Railway constantly arrived, unloading even more people into the town which added to the confusion. There were so many people here: farmers, merchants, housewives, and children.

Will spent the whole day trying to sign on with a reputable wagon master, which turned out to be a tortuous job. Hundreds of men preyed on the unsuspecting travelers, and pretty much anyone who could tell a good story was claiming the title "wagon master." Fortunately, Will possessed the name of a good man. Mr. Twitchell was a captain in the Mexican-American war and spent a good deal of time out West. Following that war, he ran many a wagon train carrying men and supplies to feed the gold rush. Too old now to fight the current war and openly proclaiming that his sympathies lay with the South, he led travelers westward fleeing Missouri to escape the atrocities being committed by the Union armies.

Will finally found him near the river port. "Mr. Twitchell, my name is William Hunter from Mexico, Missouri. My wife is Sarah Talbot. I understand your family and hers go back a long way."

Mr. Twitchell, a short, stocky man, extended his hand and answered, "Glad to meet you, William. I received a letter last week from my brother telling me that you and your wife and family were coming to St. Joe and that you would like to join us."

"That's exactly right, sir," replied Will, "but unfortunately, I'm new to all this traveling and have never stepped foot outside of Audrain County my entire life, until now. I'm willing to pull my own weight and do whatever it takes to get my family out of here into the safety of California."

"Well, William, welcome aboard," stated Mr. Twitchell. "I understand you've already purchased a wagon and a team. That's the easy part. Now I'm going to give you a list of what you're going to need in the way of supplies to make this trip. Understand, it won't be easy; everyone, including the women, will play a role in getting us to our destination. Also, it won't be cheap. To purchase a wagon, team, and supplies averages around $1,500.

James Michael Pasley

Twitchell continued, "First on your list should be good shoes because no one rides, everyone walks. The amount of supplies needed takes up all the room in the wagons, so we simply can't allow that space to be used for passengers. I've taken the liberty of writing down all the other things you'll need. Bear in mind that the bed of these wagons is only 4' x 10', and the most you will be able to haul is around 1,500 pounds. Any more than that and the teams can't handle it, especially when we get to the mountains. One big mistake you see around here is wagons with a big water barrel strapped to the side. A barrel of water weighs nearly 300 pounds. There will be plenty of water along the trail. One third of the trip follows the Platte River, and nearly all the camps we stop at are set up along rivers or springs. So, forget the water barrel, but get everything else I have listed. We leave at first light day after tomorrow, so you better get busy."

"Thank you, sir," Mr. Hunter responded. "As for supplies, I've already started. Back home I picked up a copy of that book written by U.S. Army Captain Randolph P. Marcy called "The Prairie Traveler." Looks like it has a lot of good information, and with your list, I'm sure we'll have everything we need. See you on Tuesday morning."

Will returned to the hotel and met up with his wife and the girls. "Good news, girls," said Will. "I found Mr. Twitchell, and he agreed to allow us to join his wagon train. So, now the real work begins. We leave the day after tomorrow, and we have to purchase everything we need and loaded into the wagon ready to go at first light on Tuesday. I put together a long list of supplies we still need to acquire, and we'll divide it up amongst us so we can get it all done. Mr. Twitchell told me that the trip from here to California will take a minimum of 110 days, so we are going to need a lot of supplies."

Matt, Lizzie, Will, and Sarah gathered around a small table in the room and reviewed the list:

150 pounds of flour

25 pounds of bacon or pork

15 pounds of coffee

25 pounds of sugar; also yeast, salt, pepper, and baking powder.

"Mr. Twitchell stated that when we get to Salt Lake City, we may be able to buy additional supplies but not to count on it," asserted Will.

"He also instructed how you ladies need to get appropriate clothes for this trip."

Matt and Lizzie each raised an eyebrow and asked, "What does he deem appropriate?"

"Cotton and linen fabrics don't work to protect the body against the direct rays of the sun at midday nor against rains or sudden changes in temperature," Will responded. "So, the best material is wool, and everything you wear should be made of wool, if possible."

"Good grief!" shouted the girls. "We will look like a bunch of peasant farmers everywhere we go!"

Sarah stepped in and reminded the girls that they will be on the Oregon Trail, not attending socials in downtown Kansas City. Will continued, "You will need a coat, and it should be short and bulky, red or blue flannel shirts, and pants made of thick and soft woolen material. You'll also need wool socks and stout boots that come up to your knees."

"Boots that come up to our knees!" shouted the girls. "Absolutely not!"

"Well, have it your way," remarked Will. "Mr. Twitchell says that's the best way to keep from getting bit by a rattlesnake." The girls looked at each other, and without saying a word, they knew that the reality of this trip was about to begin.

"We all are in need of purchasing good hats," Will went on. "The sun will be relentless in the summer, and when we reach the mountains, we will be walking through snow. We also need to purchase bedding for each of us. Every person should have two blankets, a comforter, a pillow, and a canvas cloth to spread on the ground."

"Won't we be sleeping in the wagon, Paw?" asked Lizzie. "No, dear. The wagon will be completely full of supplies; we will sleep on the ground," replied Will.

Matt then asked, "If the wagon is full of supplies, how will we ride?"

Aunt Sarah took this question. "We don't ride," she said. "We walk."

The girls were astonished. "Are you joshing? You expect us to walk to California?" exclaimed Matt. "That's right, girls," responded Sarah. "That is why you need good shoes. You will be walking 15 to 20 miles a day."

"While we're on the subject, you each need to purchase a canvas sack. As you are walking, you will be collecting buffalo chips," added Will.

Lizzie asked, "What's that?"

"Buffalo poop!" declared Matt.

"Why in the world would we collect buffalo poop?" asked Lizzie.

Again, Sarah stepped in to answer. "There are no trees on the prairie, so, there is no wood for cooking. You girls will collect buffalo chips as we travel across the plains, and at the end of the day, we will use them to make a fire and cook our meals." The girls snickered but soon realized that Sarah was not joking. This truly was going to be an adventure.

Rocheport, Boone County, Missouri

Having fled Huntsville, Bill and the boys rode into the small Missouri River town of Rocheport. The location for the town was noted in the journals of Lewis and Clark. In the early 1830s, with a population of just 500, the town was established with several buildings along the riverfront.

As they rode down First Street, the guerrillas robbed all the Union stores in town, and when they were finished, the boys drank the saloons dry. Bill declared the town his Confederate capital. Docked at the pier was the steamboat, *Buffington*. The guerrillas threw the captain and crew off the boat, stoked up the boilers, and churned up and down the Missouri River to the delight of the Southern townsfolk. Bill even sent off a note to Jeff Davis, informing him that the guerrillas now had a Confederate Navy in Missouri.

The next day, the steamboat, *Yellowstone*, pulled up to the pier unaware that the town was captured by the guerrillas. Bill Anderson and his men opened fire on the unsuspecting captain and crew. Fortunately, the boat was not tied off yet and was able to back away and make its escape downstream. The captain immediately proceeded to Jefferson City and reported to the Union command there the details of what happened.

The Union closed all traffic on the Missouri River between Jefferson City and Kansas City. When the Rebels heard about the closure, they proceeded to ride out into the countryside and tear down every telegraph line they could find, effectively cutting off all communication between Union headquarters in Jeff City and the Union forts on the western border.

Using Rocheport as their base of operations, the guerrillas set out to wreak havoc on the citizens of central Missouri.

Josiah and the boys sat patiently about 50 yards into the woods off the main road between Fayette and Boonville. Bill looked at Josiah and gave the order: "Same as always— wait for my signal." After a short time, the stagecoach could be seen coming down the road. When it reached the right point, Bill winked at Josiah, and all 10 of the men pulled their pistols and crashed forward through the brush. The only warning the stagehands had of the impending disaster was the sound of brush slapping against the legs of the guerrillas as they approached, which is how they earned the name "bushwhackers."

Josiah was the first to hit the road and signaled the stage to stop. The driver had no choice. Josiah hollered out, "No one needs to get hurt. Step down from there, and throw your weapons on the ground." The driver and his partner did as they were told.

Bill walked up to the stage, opened the door, and told the passengers to step out. Exiting the coach were three well-dressed ladies and two men in suits. Bill reiterated, "As my man said, no one needs to get hurt, but we would appreciate you emptying your pockets and your purses to make a donation to the Southern cause." The women and one of the men complied immediately. The other man informed them that he was the sheriff from Randolph County, and he would not be robbed by a band of murdering thugs.

At once, Archie stepped forward and promptly slit the man's throat. He emptied the man's pockets and took his pocket watch and his revolver. Not finished, he scalped the man and handed the scalp to Bill saying, "This will be a good one to add to your collection. Never had a sheriff before." Indeed, Bill did keep prized scalps. The reigns to his horse were made of these grotesque souvenirs.

Jesse advanced and told the rest of the passengers, "I wish he hadn't done that. We told you we meant no harm. All the sheriff needed to do was comply with our request. His death is his own fault." While all this was taking place, the rest of the men pulled out all the passengers' luggage and helped themselves to the valuables they found.

Captain Anderson looked at the stage driver and instructed him, "You all are free to go on, but you're going to have to leave your weapons here. When you arrive at Boonville, I want you to tell the authorities there that it was none other than Bloody Bill and his boys who robbed you and that this road is no longer open to Union travelers." The driver and his partner helped the passengers aboard, climbed atop the stage, and took off, leaving the sheriff's body in the road. The guerrillas turned in the opposite direction and headed back to their base in Rocheport.

Over the next two weeks, Bill and his men made good on their promise. They robbed 13 stagecoaches and 10 supply wagons.

When word reached Boonville that Bloody Bill and his men were operating in central Missouri, it set forth a panic among the people. In Columbia, home of the University of Missouri, the citizens' home guard unit was called to active duty. The guard unit called themselves "the Tigers" and promptly barricaded the courthouse and the University building, and they built a blockhouse in the middle of Broadway at Eighth Street.

Mr. Price, the president of the Boone County Bank, learned of the fate of the bank and its president in Huntsville. Seeing the activity by the militia, he took all the money out of the bank, and with his staff, Price split it into small parcels and buried it under fence posts on his farm three miles out of town. The money remained there until the end of the war.

May 8, 1864, St. Joseph, Missouri

James Michael Pasley

Having hoped to leave at first light as planned, it took a little longer to gather the last of the supplies needed for their journey. Will sent Matt down to the riverfront to let Mr. Twitchell know that they would be a couple of hours late. Mr. Twitchell was not happy. "Young lady," he admonished, "you go back to that hotel, and tell your uncle that this is the last time I will tolerate anyone in your party being late. Let me explain this to you. Once this wagon train sets out, it will stop only when I say stop. And we will move on when I say so. If you or anyone else in this party is late and cannot move on for any reason, they will be left behind. I don't care if you are injured or sick, or simply too tired. To delay even for a short time puts the entire party at risk. We must maintain the strictest schedule. Every minute wasted pushes us closer to the winter months, and I can tell you that if we are caught in the mountains during the snowy season, we will all perish. Therefore, it is a matter of life and death for all of us that everyone sticks to the schedule."

Matt stared at Mr. Twitchell and was terrified. "What shall we do?" she cried. "Please don't leave us behind!"

Mr. Twitchell was satisfied he'd gotten his message across. "You go back and tell your uncle that we are making camp at Savannah tonight," he advised. "It is 13 miles north. He needs to leave no later than noon if he expects to join us there tonight. If he doesn't make it, we will leave without you all at first light tomorrow."

"Thank you, thank you," Matt answered gratefully. "I will tell my uncle exactly what you said, and I promise we will be in Savannah tonight." Mr. Twitchell smiled and sent her on her way.

Matt ran as fast as she could to the hotel. When she arrived, she found Lizzie, Sarah, and Will loading the last of the supplies into the wagon. Matt told Will what Mr. Twitchell said. "Good grief, girl," said her uncle. "Did he already leave? I still have to swing by the general store and pick up the flour."

"He was pulling out as we spoke, Uncle Will," answered Matt.

"Well, we'd best get moving if we want to catch up with them at Savannah tonight," replied Will.

They quickly finished loading the wagon and headed for the general store. Loading the flour only took a short time, but as they headed out on the main road to Savannah, there was no sign of Mr. Twitchell or the wagon train. The girls panicked, but Will assured them that they had plenty of time to make Savannah before nightfall.

Sure enough, they made Savannah by 6:00 that evening and joined the rest of the group. Sarah and Will looked tired when they arrived, but Lizzie and Matt were too excited even to think that they had just walked 13 miles. Little did they know that they had another 1,827 miles to go.

May 9, 1864, City of Savannah, Andrew County, Missouri (Diary)

"We are finally underway! Left St. Joe this morning at 11 o'clock, had a very pleasant day's travel. Passed through some beautiful country, such green shady woods. We had no additional wagons with us today but we are expecting to overtake some acquaintances tomorrow. This is such a lovely little town, I feel I could tarry here a long time."

Having joined Mr. Twitchell and the rest of the wagon train, they made camp and spread their bedrolls out on the ground for their first night on the trail. Around 8:00 a.m., Mr. Twitchell came around and told everyone to finish up their coffee and breakfast. They would all be pulling out in one hour. Matt and Lizzie finished their biscuits, and then they helped Sarah clean up camp and stow everything in the wagon. Will, in the meantime, hooked up the team. At 9:00 a.m. sharp, they fell in line and set off.

FORT SCOTT KANSAS, UNION HEADQUARTERS, DISTRICT OF KANSAS

Union General John Schofield looked at the men around the table he called together. "Gentlemen, I've had enough. I am tired of your excuses, and we're going to settle the issue of dealing with these guerrillas once and for all." Seated at the table were Major Emory Foster of the 7th Missouri State Militia Cavalry, General Fitz Henry Warren of the First Iowa Cavalry, and Brigadier General James Blunt, Commander of the Department of Kansas.

General Schofield got up and walked across the room to a large map on the wall. "Major Foster, I want you to take your 800 men out of Lexington and head south for Lone Jack in Southeast Jackson County, Missouri. General Warren, you take your men and meet up with Major Foster at Lone Jack by coming up from the south. General Blunt, you will then proceed eastward from here with your cavalry and infantry divisions. With these combined forces, you are to move northwesterly from Lone Jack and press Quantrill and his guerrillas against the Missouri River."

Major Foster asked, "It looks like a good plan, General, but as we push northwesterly, how will we keep the guerrillas from fleeing west before they get to the river?" General Schofield considered this for a minute and then stated, "I will dispatch Colonel John Burris to bring his forces from Fort Leavenworth to keep the guerrillas from fleeing in that direction. This will put a total of 3,000 men at your disposal, gentlemen. I expect you to rendezvous at Lone Jack in three days' time and commence operations. We will have the enemy completely surrounded. Do not fail me. Dismissed."

Lone Jack, Missouri. Three days later

Union Major Foster already arrived with his 800 men out of Lexington the previous evening. Lone Jack was a small town of a few hundred people. Main Street consisted of a general store, a small hotel and saloon, and a livery stable. Most of the people lived on small farms in the surrounding area. Having set up camp at the west end of Main Street, Major Foster and his men turned in for the night. Foster went to bed wondering what had gone wrong with the plan so far. Generals Blunt and Warren should have been here. Once again, communication among the Union troops was a disaster. Every time a new telegraph line was strung, the guerrillas would tear it down within two days.

At 5:30 the next morning, Major Foster was awakened by the sound of gunfire. As he jumped from his bedroll, his second-in-command, Lieutenant Mike Matney, burst into the major's tent and reported, "Major, we are being overrun by the enemy!" Foster grabbed his hat, strapped on his pistol, and asked, "Lieutenant, how many are there, and what is their current location?"

"Sir, it appears it is a huge force of almost 1,500 men," Matney replied. "Our pickets were able to drive them to one side of Main Street, and we have now occupied the other side and holed up in the general store and livery stable."

As he stepped out into the early morning sunlight, Major Foster gave the command, "Lieutenant, take several men and bring our cannon forward. We'll play hell driving those boys out of the buildings with just rifles, but that 12-pounder will be a big equalizer even though we are outnumbered." Lieutenant Matney saluted and headed off to carry out his orders while Major Foster turned and sprinted toward Main Street.

The battle lasted for several hours, and Lieutenant Matney and his men displayed tremendous courage by riding through the withering fire straight up Main Street and manning the gun, firing several rounds into the adjacent buildings. The guerrillas quickly concentrated their fire on the artillery crew, driving them off the big gun. Josiah was among the first to reach the cannon, and he and Cole quickly turned the big gun on the Union forces. This scene was played out several times during the battle with both sides utilizing the sole piece of artillery in the conflict. During one exchange, Lieutenant Matney was hit in the leg and fell next to the gun unable to continue in the fight. Josiah saw Matney lying there and submitted, "Son, I saw what you did, bringing this cannon out here at the beginning of the fight. You've done your part. Just lie there and don't give me no trouble, and I'll let you live." The young officer, having lost a lot of blood, nodded at Josiah and curled up behind the ammo box.

As the battle raged on, Major Foster continue to look down the road for Generals Blunt and Warren along with their forces. They never came. Completely outnumbered and running low on ammunition, Foster and his men had no choice but to give up the fight and retreat.

When the smoke cleared, Major Foster's forces reportedly suffered nearly 300 casualties. Josiah and the guerrillas suffered 110. It was a stroke of luck that, as Josiah, Bloody Bill, and the boys were fleeing the area south of Boonville several days earlier, they met up with Colonels John T. Coffee and Gideon W. Thompson, who recruited over 1,000 Missouri boys to join the Confederate cause.

The guerrillas set about tending to their wounded, and as they walked the battlefield, Josiah came upon Lieutenant Matney still huddled next to the ammo box. Josiah called out to Bloody Bill, "Hey Bill! This here is that crazy Yankee that rode out right at the beginning of the battle, dragging this cannon over here."

"Is he dead?" Bill wanted to know.

Josiah hollered back, "No, just hit in the leg. What do we want to do with him?"

Archie heard the conversation and asked, "Can I have him?"

Anderson just smiled at Archie and said, "Not yet. I have a plan for that boy."

Meanwhile, Josiah helped Lieutenant Matney to the front porch of the hotel and saw to it that his wound was tended to.

That evening, as they sat around the campfire, Josiah asked Bill, "What you plan on doing with that Yankee lieutenant?"

Bill reached into his saddlebag and pulled out the Kansas City newspaper and tossed it to Josiah. On the front page, Bill circled an article, stating that Perry Hoy, a Confederate guerrilla, was captured and was being held at Fort Leavenworth. It went on to say that he would be executed the following Monday. Bill said, "Perry is a good man, and I've known him and his family since I was a kid. Tomorrow morning, I'm going to send a message by rider to that newspaper and let them know that we have Lieutenant Matney and would be willing to trade him for Perry."

The following morning, Bloody Bill sent the rider into town to see if an exchange could be made. Late that afternoon, the rider returned to their camp, dismounted, and approached Captain Anderson. "Well, what did they say?" Bill inquired. The rider looked down, shuffled his feet a bit, and then replied, "Bill, I hate to tell you this, but when I got there, they just laughed and told me to tell you they went ahead and hanged Perry day before yesterday."

Bill stared at the man with a cold, icy gaze, and without taking his eyes off him shouted, "Archie, go fetch the prisoner."

Josiah stepped forward and said, "Bill, let's think about this. I liked your idea of keeping this guy alive, so we could exchange him. Why not keep him alive a while longer in case someone else gets caught?"

Anderson looked at Josiah with the same icy stare and asked, "Since when do you care about these damned Yankees?"

Josiah stammered slightly and told Bloody Bill that he promised Lieutenant Matney if he didn't cause any trouble during the battle, he would let him live.

Bill just smiled a sinister smile and retorted, "You made that promise, not me." He then turned to Archie and said, "Grab a shovel and fetch the prisoner."

Bill and Archie marched Lieutenant Matney out of camp to a small clearing in the woods. At gunpoint, they forced the lieutenant to dig his own grave. Bill then asked, "Do you have any last words?"

Lieutenant Matney stood tall and looked Bill in the eye. "All I ask is that you keep that crazy little bastard away from my body when the deed has been done."

Archie just smiled. Bill looked at Matney and said, "Lieutenant, I saw what you did out there this morning. You're a brave man, and Josiah told me of the promise he made to you. I wish I could honor that promise, but this war and your army have killed a lot of good, brave men. I believe in an eye for an eye. To not respond in kind to your people for what they did to my friend Perry Hoy would be a mistake. The best I can do is promise you that I will not let Archie touch you when we're done." With that, Bill pulled his pistol and shot the lieutenant squarely between the eyes. He fell back into the open grave, and Bill turned to Archie and gave him an order. "Archie, that is a promise I aim to keep. I wish we had more men like him fighting for our side. Fill that grave and join us back at camp."

Archie frowned, saluted Bill, and muttered, "Yes, sir." He then went to work shoveling.

NODAWAY RIVER, MAY 10, 1864 (DIARY)

"We left beautiful Savannah early this morning and have traveled nearly 30 miles. Have now encamped for the first night on the banks of the Nodaway River. It is the most beautiful country around here I've ever seen, such beautiful green trees and such gentle sloping hills. Indeed I'm perfectly delighted so far, this is a perfect paradise. I could live here always. We had supper early, had no great difficulty in cooking for the first time. There are 10 wagons here with us tonight and some very pleasant people. But still each day I am getting still further away from my home and my loved ones there. It is getting late we must soon retire. I almost hate to think of losing time and sleep at this spot. The moon will shine so pretty and everything seems so beautiful here."

May 19, 1864 (Diary)

"Another beautiful day though quite warm. Camped again on the bank of the same little stream, so muddy not so pretty here as last night. All Black Republicans I suppose in this section, though such beautiful country, still in Holt County. News reached us late this evening that Lincoln had called for 400,000 men. Oh how I wonder where Josiah is and if he is safe."

(Author's note: Matt's reference to black Republicans goes back to 1854 when the Republican Party was founded. Southern Republican Party members were called "black" Republicans to identify them as proponents of black equality. During the 1860 elections, Southern Democrats used the term derisively to press their belief that Abraham Lincoln's victory would incite slave rebellions in the South.)

Matt and her party crossed the Missouri River at Nebraska City and set out across the seemingly never-ending prairie. Sure enough, they found no wood with which to cook. Lizzie and Matt pulled their canvas bags from the wagon and started collecting buffalo chips. As they walked along, Lizzie said, "This is kind of like an Easter egg hunt."

Matt looked at her cousin incredulously and remarked, "I don't know where you've been celebrating Easter, but these don't look like any eggs I ever collected." Both girls giggled.

Sarah heard them laughing and asked, "What's so funny?" When the girls told her, she said, "Here's an idea. Why don't the two of you have a contest to see who can collect the most 'Easter eggs?' The loser has to build the fire and help with the cooking."

"That's a great idea!" Lizzie affirmed. With that, she took off running, hoping to win the contest.

Matt smiled at her aunt and said, "Pretty clever. You know I don't mind building a fire and cooking, but I hate collecting buffalo chips. Looks like a win for all of us."

Sarah looked at Matt and said, "You're learning, young lady!"

10 MILES SOUTH OF THE CITY OF FAYETTE, HOWARD COUNTY, MISSOURI

Bill, Josiah, and the rest of the men made camp along a small stream just south of the city of Fayette. It was midday, and they decided to stop long enough to refill their canteens, take a short break, then head on to the farm of their good friend Bill Brown. They knew he and his wife Gloria were good Confederate sympathizers and would put them up in their barn for the evening where they could make plans for their upcoming raid on the town of Fayette.

News of the boys' raid on Huntsville, Missouri, put the Union forces hot on their trail. Union patrols were sent out to scour the countryside and bring the guerrillas to justice. These patrols were made up of Kansas troops known as Jennison's Jayhawkers.

When the Civil War officially started, abolitionists from Kansas, who had been fighting Missourians for the past five years, formally joined up with the Union. One particular group made up of murderers and thieves came to Mound City, Kansas, upon hearing that war broke out, and they immediately enlisted.

They became the Seventh Kansas Volunteer Cavalry, and their commander was Dr. Charles Jennison. The doctor was born in New York and raised in Wisconsin, where he studied and practiced medicine. He moved to Mound City, Kansas, in 1857 and formed his own vigilante committee, which gained fame in 1860 by hanging two Missourians caught trying to recover their slaves that were stolen by Kansas abolitionists.

Jennison was a highly intelligent egomaniac. He was also an excellent horse thief. When people in Kansas were checking on the pedigree of a fine horse, the sellers would often joke that "this horse came out of Missouri by Jennison."

Jennison was a staunch abolitionist, and with his background, he was a natural choice to become captain of the Seventh Kansas Cavalry. The unit adopted the name Jayhawk, claiming they were like hawks who could swoop down on unsuspecting and less capable Blue Jays, a type of bird notorious for raiding the nests of other birds.

Taking advantage of the defenseless border between Missouri and Kansas, the Jayhawks wreaked havoc on the Missourians, just as they had done since 1856. The big difference now was that they were riding for the Union, and they could punish Missourians under the guise of merely claiming they were carrying out the orders of their military commanders. Wherever they rode in Missouri, they left behind a trail of revenge, murder, looting, and arson.

Josiah and Frank set up in the woods along the road about 100 yards from camp. It was their turn to stand guard while the rest of the men took a break. After about 30 minutes, Frank signaled Josiah and pointed up the road. Heading in their direction, they saw a Union patrol of 20 men. Frank pulled his rifle while Josiah mounted his horse and rode off in the direction of camp to warn the others. Shortly after, as Josiah rode into camp, the first shot was fired. He could tell from the sound that it was Frank firing his Sharps rifle. Immediately, he heard the return fire of the Union soldiers who took cover in the woods alongside the road. Bill's men mounted up, and as they headed out, Frank joined them and declared, "That was fun, but I don't think those boys are too happy with us. We'd best get moving."

The Union patrol remained in the cover of the trees for about 10 minutes when their commander, Patrick O'rourke, gave the all clear and told the men to mount up. Captain O'Rourke knew the area well, having grown up in Fayette, and he knew that farmer Brown was the most prominent Rebel in the area. With this knowledge, he headed straight for the Brown farm.

It took Captain O'rourke and his men only about an hour to reach the farm. As they approached, there was no sign of life. He gave the signal to his men to surround the farmhouse. He and his lieutenant rode up to the front of the house, dismounted, and stepped onto the front porch. Captain O'rourke shouted, "Brown, come out of there! I know you are home. We mean you and your missus no harm, but we are here on official business and if need be will kick the door in."

Immediately, a shot rang out from inside the farmhouse through the front door and entered squarely into the chest of Captain O'rourke, who fell dead. The lieutenant reached for his pistol, but he as well was too late as dozens of shots rang out. Wounded in the leg, the lieutenant dove into the bushes off the front porch. The Union soldiers dismounted and took up positions surrounding the house, finding what cover they could.

As they opened fire, women and children could be heard screaming inside the house, so, the lieutenant called to his men to cease firing. When they did, several women and children came out; once clear of the house, the fight resumed. Under covering fire, two soldiers ran forward and pulled the lieutenant to safety. He looked at the women and children and demanded, "Who's in there?" The youngest of the women glared at the young officer and answered, "You might as well give up right now; it's Bloody Bill and his men, and they'll kill every one of you. They will not give up."

The lieutenant replied, "We'll see about that. Boys, set that house afire, and let's flush those rats out of there." Two of the soldiers went into the barn and gathered some rags, a few sticks, and some kerosene. With torches in hand, they mounted up, rode to the house, and set it afire. The lieutenant smiled and told his men, "Sit back boys, we're going to watch those Rebels roast in hell."

Inside the house, Josiah and the boys knew they were in big trouble. The clapboard house was quickly engulfed in flames. Bill looked at Josiah and said, "What you think?"

"Well, we obviously can't stay here!" Josiah snapped. About that time, Jesse hollered from the kitchen at the back of the house that the rear wall was about to go. Josiah joined him and looked out the window through the billowing smoke and could see there were only two soldiers between them and the woods at the rear of the house.

He shouted to Bill: "There's only two of them back here, and there's 10 of us."

"I like those odds!" Bloody Bill Anderson replied, and without hesitation, he and his boys ran for the back of the house, kicked open the rear door, and opened fire. The two soldiers fell immediately, and Bill and the boys ran past them deep into the woods. The Union soldiers saw what happened and turned to the lieutenant for orders.

The lieutenant looked at the situation and told the men, "Boys, I'm as tough as any man, but I also know that to chase Rebels into the woods is suicide. They live there."

"But, sir," said one of the soldiers, "they are on foot."

"I know that," the lieutenant answered, "but they are now like wounded animals, and it will take a lot more than just us to flush them out of there. By the time we get reinforcements here, they will be long gone. They'll split up, steal horses from the surrounding farms, and meet up again at the farm of another Rebel sympathizer 20 miles from here by tomorrow. That is why they call them gray ghosts." The lieutenant was exactly right.

MAY 30, 1864, NEBRASKA TERRITORY (DIARY)

"*The weather is still beautiful. Been washing today for the first time since we started to California. On the banks of Bear Creek. Some other trains have overtaken us, and they are here tonight, about 100 men. Several of the men claim they have seen Indians in the hills and they appear to be following us. We are in the open plains far from timber and water. Had to bring both with us from the last camping place. It is raining. The first shower since we started just two weeks ago. I dreamed of Josiah last night. May God bless him though I may never see him again. There was a dance last night by starlight. The girls danced without hoops. Dr. Dobbins played the violin. We were up till late. A great many attended the dance here on Bear Creek. We have not been troubled yet by Indians or robbers. God grant we may get safely to our place of destination.*"

Matt was startled awake by the sound of rifle shots. Uncle Will came running and called out, "Girls, get on the other side of the wagon with Sarah, and take cover."

All the teams were unhitched at the end of the day's travel, and the wagons were pushed into a large circle. As was the common practice, the livestock was confined inside this circle since there was no corral to put them in or trees to tie them up at the end of the day. For this reason, everyone slept on the outside of the makeshift corral.

Mr. Twitchell called out to the menfolk and told them all to take up positions. "The Indians will not attack us," he said, "but they are lobbing arrows into the corral in hopes of killing our livestock. They know that in the morning, we will have to move on and leave any dead animals here for them to feast on."

Matt looked behind her, and sure enough, one of the oxen in the corral lay dead on the ground. The men stood watch for the remainder of the evening, and fortunately, at first light, they could see that only one of the oxen was killed. Mr. Twitchell called the men together and lectured them. "Boys, now you can see why we form the wagons into a circle and put the livestock inside. It is also the reason why we brought along extra livestock. Those Indians out there are hungry. Ever since we forced them onto reservations and killed the buffalo, they have no way to feed their families. They are simply doing what they need to do to stay alive. Rest assured that they are not after us, they are simply trying to eat. From this point forward, we will need men to post watch every night to protect our livestock. I will set up a schedule, and we will take turns standing guard."

As they prepared to pull out the next morning, Matt and Lizzie saw Indians on the ridge above camp, mounted on their horses, waiting for the wagon train to move on.

Matt overheard Will and Sarah talking about Mr. Johnson, who had been riding ahead of the wagon train acting as a scout. Will said, "He hasn't been seen for three days, and even though Mr. Twitchell says the Indians aren't after us, it is not safe for someone to be out there alone. I sure hope he's all right."

As the wagon train pressed on toward the Platte River, they abruptly came to a halt. Will said, "You all stay here, and I will go forward to find out what's holding us up." As Will approached the front of the wagon train, he could see Mr. Twitchell and several of the men gathered around something on the road. Lying on the road was Mr. Johnson with two arrows sticking out of his chest. It looked like he had been dead for several days, and he had been scalped. There was also no sign of his horse or his rifle.

"We can't risk losing another man," Mr. Twitchell stated. "From this point forward, we will have to move on without the benefit of having a scout checking out the trail ahead. You men need to form a burial detail. It's time you all learned something else about life on the trail. When someone dies, we will take the time to give them a proper burial, but as soon as we are done, we must move on. The grave needs to be dug right here in the tracks where the wagons pass. If you bury someone off the trail, the animals will dig them up as soon as we're out of sight. By burying our casualties right here on the trail, the wagons passing over the grave will pack the soil tight and keep the predators from disturbing the final resting place of our loved ones. Get to it, men. We're wasting daylight, and I want to make the Platte River by nightfall." Mr. Twitchell turned and headed back to inform the others what occurred.

Sarah, Lizzie, and Matt were terrified when they heard the news. Uncle Will returned and assured them that if they stayed with the group and didn't venture out alone, they would be fine.

After about an hour, the burial detail finished their work, and the wagon train rolled forward over the freshly dug grave of Mr. Johnson.

CITY OF FAYETTE, HOWARD COUNTY, MISSOURI

Josiah, Bill, and the men made camp in the hills overlooking the city of Fayette. After supper, they sat around the campfire to discuss their plans for the next day. Just after they sat down, Frank James hollered out, "Rider approaching!" The men took up positions and drew their pistols. As the rider rode into camp, he was quickly surrounded. Anderson looked up at the man and exclaimed, "Well, as I live and breathe! I figured once you got married, we'd never see you again." It was none other than Captain Quantrill. He dismounted, shook hands with Bill, and said, "I heard you boys were in the area, and I couldn't just sit home and let you have all the fun." Bill said," We were just sittin' down getting ready to discuss our plan for tomorrow."

"Well, I'd love to hear it," Quantrill responded. He then joined the others at the campfire. The James boys and the Youngers were thrilled to see their former leader and asked about his new married life.

Captain Quantrill told the men that he'd met his wife while he was conducting raids in Jackson County. Her name was Kate Clarke. Clarke was Quantrill's middle name, and it was later said that her real name was Kate King. Very little was known about her. Some say she came from a wealthy family, but others said she was a woman of low character and was a madam at a house of ill repute in Kansas City. Of course, no one would ever say that to Quantrill's face and live to talk about it. Ever since he married Kate, he lived in hiding, so the boys were truly glad to see him.

Bill turned to Captain Quantrill and said, "We're planning on raiding Fayette tomorrow. I understand that the Union has a patrol stationed there, and they are using the courthouse as a headquarters and the town as a supply depot for all the other patrols in the area. I also understand that there is a nice bank in that town, and with the way the war is going, it can't hurt to build up our nest egg, so we have something to live on when this war comes to an end."

Quantrill looked at Josiah and asked, "What do you think?"

"Well, Captain, we are short on supplies, and I hear tell that only 20 men are protecting that town."

Quantrill stared at both men and offered, "Therein lies the problem. Those 20 soldiers are holed up in a brick courthouse on the town square. Trust me, I have attacked brick courthouses in the past. Every time, we took a terrible beating. I remember attacking the courthouse in Lamar, Missouri. There were only 15 Union soldiers in that courthouse, and they only had single shot rifles. But they had 50 of them, and they had preloaded every last one of them, so when the fight started, they fired and kept on firing. We lost eight good men that day and tried again a second day only to lose another three."

"By God, Captain. I can't believe that you are saying this," Anderson interjected. "If I didn't know better, I'd say that marriage has caused you to lose your nerve." Only Bloody Bill could say this to Quantrill.

He glared at Bill with his steely blue eyes and retorted, "There is a fine line between losing your nerve and just being stupid. If you raid that town tomorrow, it will be one of the dumbest things you've ever done, and you will take casualties." With that, Quantrill got up, walked to his horse, mounted up, and departed. "I wish you boys luck tomorrow; you're going to need it."

Josiah turned to Bill and asked, "What you think?"

"I think that man has been out of the game too long. We ride at first light. Get some rest."

Early the next morning, Josiah, Bill, and the rest of the men broke camp and headed for Fayette. They brought additional forces from Rocheport and recruited several good Southern men from the surrounding area, bringing their strength to 65 men.

Bill gave the order to attack as he and his men rode up Church Street. They broke into a gallop and let out a Rebel yell as they rode into the courthouse square. Immediately, they were met by a volley from 30 men of the 9th Cavalry, who barricaded themselves in the courthouse and a railroad tie blockhouse on the hill next to Central Methodist College. The guerrillas stepped into a hornets' nest. There were more troops stationed in Fayette than they anticipated.

The Union forces held their fire until the guerrillas were right at the steps of the courthouse. Between the shots coming from within and the gunfire blasting from the railroad tie blockhouse, the guerrillas found themselves in a deadly crossfire and had no choice but to turn and ride back down Church Street through the gauntlet of enemy fire. The fight ended quickly. Thirteen guerrillas lay dead in the street, and another 30 were wounded, slumped in their saddles, as they rode out of town.

The men regrouped at the campsite where they stayed the night before. Quantrill was there waiting for them, and when Bill rode up, he reprimanded Anderson. "Bill, look what you've done. If you are going to command this unit, you need to realize the decisions you make mean life and death for these boys. I tried to warn you, but you just wouldn't listen. Take a look at your wounded. Half of them won't live through the night. Pride is a terrible thing to have to deal with. For the sake of your men, I hope you've learned something here today." Quantrill jumped on his horse and rode away. That was the last time he and Bloody Bill ever saw one another.

As Bill surveyed the damage, he knew the captain was right. To be wounded in this war was sometimes worse than being killed outright. Ever since that Frenchman, Claude Minie, invented the new bullet in use, chances of surviving a gunshot wound were slim to none. The Minie ball was accurate and carried one tremendous wallop. If it hit anywhere in the torso, it was a kill shot. The victims may not die instantly, but they would die. If it hit an arm or leg, it did not simply break the bone, it shattered it. The doctors would have no choice but to amputate the limb.

Many times after a battle, as one walked among the casualties, one could see that their coats were pulled open. For the longest time, Bill thought this was because fellow soldiers were trying to identify the dead. In reality, as men were shot on the field of battle, they immediately pulled open their coats to see if the round hit them in the torso. If it did, they knew they were doomed. Josiah walked through camp and was devastated by what he saw. *"That could have been me,"* he thought.

About that time, Jesse walked up to him and stated, "Josiah, I have to tell you, that was the most scared I have ever been in my life."

Josiah looked at his friend and quietly stated, "Me too, Jesse, me too."

JUNE 14, 1864, BANKS OF THE PLATTE RIVER. NEBRASKA TERRITORY (DIARY)

"*Another day on the Platte. Still we are not crossed. Saw some people passing on their way to Nevada and with them one of my old acquaintances, Kate Clarke. I rode with her down to our camp. How tearing it is to meet with a friend sometimes, especially here on the plains. I talked till late tonight with Kate Clarke. Slept with her in her wagon. They had music in their camp which was very nice.*"

As all the wagons camped along the banks of the Platte River waiting for the ferry to take them across, Matt and Lizzie walked among the various camps to see if they saw anyone they knew. Someone shouted, "Matt Logan!" Matt turned, and standing before her was her old friend Kate Clarke. The girls embraced each other. Matt turned to her cousin and gushed, "Lizzie, I want you to meet one of my best friends from back home. She and I went to school together. This is Kate Clarke."

"Pleased to meet you, Kate," greeted Lizzie. Matt looked at Kate and asked, "What in the world are you doing way out here? Last I heard, you married that handsome Captain Quantrill."

"That's true," Kate replied. "With things as crazy as they are back home, William thought it best that I go visit my parents for a while until things calm down. As you know, the local Provost Marshal is hunting down all the guerrillas' families and taking out his anger on them. My mother and father live just 10 miles up the trail here, and I decided to hitch a ride with my sister's family who are headed on to Nevada to stay with her in-laws until things calm down. Why don't you and Lizzie come over to our camp tonight and have supper with us? Some of the menfolk will be playing music. It will be a great opportunity to catch up."

"I'll have to check with my Aunt Sarah and Uncle Will to see if it's permitted, but I would love to come back and visit," Matt replied.

Kate turned to head back to her camp and offered an invitation. "By all means, you tell your aunt and uncle that they are more than welcome to join us. We have plenty of food, and my brother-in-law makes the best damn moonshine this side of the Mississippi."

"That will clinch the deal!" Matt exclaimed. "Uncle Will never gives up a chance to sample good moonshine. See you tonight!"

The girls headed back to camp and told Will and Sarah about the invitation. They both agreed it would be fun, and Sarah declared, "Girls, let's get busy and bake some fresh bread that we can take to our hosts tonight."

The girls quickly pitched in, and before they knew it, it was time for them to go see Kate. When they arrived at Kate's camp, her brother-in-law shook hands with Will and stated," Glad to meet you. My name is Sam Miller. I understand you're quite the connoisseur when it comes to Missouri whiskey."

Will laughed and retorted, "I don't know about that, but I know our ancestors all came from Kentucky to Missouri, and nobody makes better whiskey than the folks back home."

"Well, then I think you're going to like this," Sam offered. "My parents also came out of Kentucky, and my paw taught me everything he knows. We been living in Jackson County ever since I was a little boy. So, there you have it. Missouri whiskey with a Kentucky background; let's give it a try." Sam grabbed a jug out of the back of the wagon with a couple of tin cups, and the two men sat next to the fire.

Shortly after that, the women told the men the food was ready and to come and get it. Kate and her sister spread the food out on the tailgate of the wagon, and everyone helped themselves. When the meal was done, Matt and Lizzie cleaned up everything for Kate and her sister and told them to go sit by the fire with the men; they'd be along shortly. Lizzie and Matt finished their chores quickly and joined the rest of the group.

Sarah turned to Kate as they sat by the fire and remarked, "I can't thank you all enough. I've been cooking for this bunch every night since we left. It sure was nice to just simply walk over here and have a great meal. You all shouldn't have."

"Don't be ridiculous," replied Kate. "We brought way more supplies than we needed to get to my folks' house. It would've gone to waste if you hadn't come over."

"I don't believe that for a minute, but again, thank you so much for having us over tonight."

As they settled in for the evening, about 20 other members of the camp showed up. One fellow pulled out a fiddle, and another started playing the harmonica. With that, the party started. Everyone was enjoying the evening, and after about an hour, Kate and Matt slipped away to the other side of the wagon where they could sit and talk.

"Kate," Matt said, hoping to learn good news. "Please tell me you have news on Josiah. I've been worried sick about him ever since we left."

Kate replied, "Well, Matt, here's what I know. Josiah, Bill, and the boys are giving those Union soldiers a run for their money. Last I heard, they set up their headquarters in Rocheport, and they were all fine. They've been conducting raids on supply lines between the Union forts. In addition to that, they've torn down all the telegraph lines and cut off communications from St. Louis Union headquarters to all of the other forces scattered throughout the state. I think the boys are really enjoying themselves. Every time they rob a wagon train full of supplies, they not only get food and clothing but all the best weapons. I hear tell that in addition to brand-new Navy Colt revolvers, they are also carrying those new Sharps rifles and have all the ammunition they could ever need. William claims he can hit a target 500 yards out with that new rifle, and all the boys have one," Kate informed Matt.

"On one of the last raids, along with the supplies, they captured a hospital wagon filled with everything they would ever need if one of them were to get injured or sick," Kate continued. "The biggest prize of all has been that every time they raid a wagon train, the military correspondence is aboard. It not only tells them when the next wagon train will be headed down their way, but it also lets them know where the Union soldiers are stationed, how many there are, and what their orders are for operations in that area. They even have the latest passwords being used by the patrols!"

"Do you have any idea how long ago it was that they were in Rocheport?" Matt asked.

"The information I have is about three weeks old," Kate declared. "I heard it straight from my husband, so I know it is true. Being their former captain, he has been keeping tabs on them, and you know he has always loved Josiah like a brother. He told me when

I left that he was headed over toward Fayette where he heard Josiah and the rest of the boys are camped, planning a raid on the city of Fayette. I wish I knew more, but at this point, all we can do is hope and pray that we see our menfolk safe and sound again shortly." Then she added, "We'd best get back to the festivities, or they will come looking for us." The girls then headed back to join the others.

The party lasted late into the evening, and when it finally broke up, everyone exchanged handshakes and hugs and wished each other well and safe travels. As Matt lay in her bedroll that night and looked up at the full moon, she couldn't help but think of Josiah, wondering if he was safe and looking up at the same evening sky.

JUNE 23, 1864. CITY OF RENICK, MISSOURI

After the disaster at Fayette, Bloody Bill and the men decided to stick with tried-and-true tactics. No more brick courthouses. He and the guerrillas decided to attack the Missouri Railroad station at Renick, Missouri, in Randolph County. They rode into town early that morning and set fire to the train station after robbing the bank. The telegraph was located in the station. Off in the distance, they heard a train whistle, and as the train rounded the bend in the distance and approached the town, Bill and the Confederates quickly pulled down all the telegraph lines, mounted up, and fled toward Rocheport.

Just as they expected, the train was filled with Union soldiers. On board was Major Brad Frazier and the Seventh Illinois Cavalry, who took the train from Macon, Missouri, heading down to Columbia. As the train came to a stop, the major ordered the men to unload the horses from the baggage cars immediately and mount up. The men did as they were ordered, and very quickly, the Seventh Illinois set off in hot pursuit of the guerrillas who had just set fire to the town. Frank and Josiah set up as pickets high on the ridge outside of town and observed the Union forces preparing their pursuit. They caught up with Bloody Bill and let him know that the Yankees were coming with about 30 men. Bill led his men to a spot another two miles down the road where it narrowed and

James Michael Pasley

cut through a forest.

"You boys know the drill. Take up positions on either side of the road, and wait for my signal," Bill ordered. With that, the men split up 10 to each side and waited deep in the woods for the approaching soldiers led by Frazier. They didn't have to wait long. As the patrol approached the designated point in the road, Bill let out a whistle, and both groups of guerrillas came bursting out of the woods and opened fire on their unsuspecting prey. Major Frazier was the first to fall from his horse. Before his men could pull their rifles, the guerrillas were on them, and each, carrying two 6-shot pistols, made quick work of killing the rest of the patrol. The guerrillas did not take a single casualty. This tactic worked time and time again. The element of surprise and the overwhelming firepower of 20 guerrillas unleashing 240 rounds in less than a minute was more than any Union patrol could handle. The guerrillas were highly mobile, to make matters worse, and were able to cover considerable distances in a very short time during their escape because they knew the countryside like the back of their hands.

The Confederates dismounted and searched the bodies for anything of value. Bill and Archie approached Frazier's body. Bill checked his coat pockets and found valuable correspondence, giving the assignments of all the other Union patrols like his and providing details of where and when they were being deployed. Bill took the information and tucked it into his hat. Archie, having just scalped two of the Union soldiers, looked at Anderson and asked, "Can I have him?"

"What do you want with him, Archie?"

Clement, with a crazed look in his eyes, told Bill, "The way I see it, you just got those orders from down south telling you that something big was coming on the east side of the state and that we were to raise as much hell over here as we can to draw those Union boys out of St. Louis. I figure the best way to do that is to scare the living daylights out of the people around here so they will be sure to demand that additional troops be sent."

Captain Anderson looked at him and said with a smile, "Archie, you are plumb crazy! I'm glad you're on our side and not the other. I don't care what you do with him, but be quick about it. There may be other patrols in the area that heard the shots and will be heading our way."

In just a few minutes, Archie said, "I'm ready to go." Bill looked at him and saw that he mounted his horse, and the Major's body was slumped over the back of it.

Bill looked at him and asked, "What are you up to?"

Archie replied, "You'll see."

The men mounted up and continued in the direction of Rocheport. When they reached the main crossroads that took the road south to Columbia or north to Moberly, Archie asked to stop. Needing to rest the horses, Bill gave the signal for the group to halt. Archie dismounted and pulled Frazier's body off the back of his horse. He then dragged it to a signpost at one of the corners of the four-way intersection. Clement leaned the major's body against the post, crossed his legs, and proceeded to cut the officer's head off and set it in his lap. He stepped back, admiring his work. Josiah looked on and said, "Archie, I'm not sure that's what they meant when they said to create a diversion, but I reckon that'll send a clear message to everyone who lives in these parts!" They all mounted up again and continued on their way.

When reports came in about multiple guerrilla attacks such as this one, Union Headquarters in St. Louis assumed that this was the work of many groups of guerrillas operating over a large area. When they thought there were up to 500 guerrillas operating, there were never more than 40 or 50 in most cases. For this reason, massive numbers of Union troops were dispatched throughout the state, hunting down guerrillas that didn't exist.

James Michael Pasley

By 1864, the Union committed more than 50,000 troops to the state of Missouri, unaware that all the troubles were being perpetrated by no more than 500 men.

For this reason, the Union command started to issue what they called General Orders, which basically made war on the citizens of Missouri. The reasoning behind this was that the guerrillas could not continue to operate if they did not have the backing of the citizens who were providing shelter and supplies for them. Missouri citizens, already living under martial law, saw all their constitutional rights cast aside as the Union military enforced these orders.

These General Orders were astounding. Back in July of 1862, Union General Schofield issued General Order 19. It stated: "Every able-bodied man capable of bearing arms and subject to military duty is hereby ordered to repair without delay to the nearest military post and report for duty in the Union Army under the commanding officer. Every man will bring with him whatever arms he may have or can procure and a good horse if he has one." The order went on to say: "The purpose of this order is to exterminate the guerrillas that infest our state." This order forced the men of the state of Missouri to make a choice. They no longer could stand on the sidelines. The federal government was declaring each citizen was either with us or against us. Any man in the state of Missouri not wearing a Union uniform immediately was seen as a guerrilla and shot on sight. Needless to say, this caused many men to leave their farms and join up with the guerrillas.

In August of the same year, General Schofield issued General Order 9. It stated: "During active operations in the field in pursuit of guerrillas, the troops of this command will not be encumbered with transportation of supplies, but will, as far as possible, obtain subsistence from the enemy and those who aid and encourage the rebellion." Union soldiers in the field held the full authorization of the federal government to pillage any home they chose throughout the state.

Guerilla Camp, 2 1/2 miles Northeast of Independence, Missouri

In the early morning, Josiah and Frank James sat near the fire waiting for the morning coffee to boil. Frank pulled a letter from his saddlebag, and as he read, Josiah could see the dour look on his face. "What's wrong, Frank? Bad news from home?"

Frank continued studying the letter and replied, "I don't see how it can get much worse. This letter is from my maw. She says that the local Provost Marshall ordered her and seven other Clay County families banished from the community. She claims that the Union troops are due to round them up tomorrow and take them to the Arkansas state line where they will be put on boats and shipped south on the White River. I can't believe they are doing this to her. That old woman and those families have done nothing wrong other than be blood kin to us Rebels." James shrugged his shoulders and, with a resigned expression on his face, continued, "I suppose it doesn't really matter at this point; we've lost everything. Back in 1862, under martial law, the Union came up with that system of loyalty oaths and performance bonds where all the people of Missouri were required to swear and sign an oath of loyalty to the U.S. Government and post a $1,000 bond. Not hardly anyone in this state can come up with $1,000, so if the Provost Marshal decides you're disloyal, he just simply takes your farm. That is exactly what he did to us. If you refused to sign the loyalty oath, you were immediately arrested and imprisoned. Break the oath, you were shot on sight."

"He has made himself a small fortune on the backs of the citizens of Missouri, and I understand every Provost Marshal in the state is doing the same thing. It doesn't matter if you're Union or Confederate, they see all Missourians as the enemy. When they confiscate your property, it goes up for sale on the courthouse steps. The Provost Marshal then places the first bid. No one in their right mind would bid against him. When a Provost Marshal sees a nice farm, he just claims the people living there are disloyal, takes their farm, and buys it for pennies on the dollar."

James Michael Pasley

Josiah couldn't believe what he was hearing and asked, "Can't anyone do anything to stop this?"

Frank just smiled and responded, "The Provost Marshall keeps the loyalty of his officers by giving a lot of these properties to them. Some entire communities have merely disappeared."

"I understand what you are saying," Josiah replied, "but how does he have the power to banish your mother?"

Frank looked at the letter again and stated: "According to this, the Provost Marshal has the full backing of the U.S. Government, under General Order #35, which gives him the power to banish people, even though no act of disloyalty can be proven. It gets even worse than that. She says here that General Schofield issued another order stating that for every Union soldier killed by us guerrillas, $5,000 will be assessed and collected from the disloyal living in the community where the death occurred. He has ordered the collection of $300,000 in northern Missouri and another $500,000 from St. Louis to feed and clothe his men. Maw also says that Union troops are raiding and looting homes and taking what they want."

Josiah just shook his head and declared, "I had no idea it'd gotten this bad. Bill just told me that we were coming to Independence to help the people who live there and that the Union was making their lives a living hell. He said Jennison's Jayhawkers and came into town about a month ago and forced all the men in town at bayonet point into the courthouse square. Then they selected a resident of the town to pick out among the men who was pro-South and who was Union. Those singled out as secessionists were forced to take an oath of allegiance to the Union, post a bond, and were then locked up in the town jail. While the men were all being held in the courthouse square, the Jayhawkers went door-to-door, having their way with the women, and robbing the town of everything not nailed down. Several homes were burned to the ground. We aim to set things right today."

LITTLEBY, MISSOURI, AUDRAIN COUNTY, LOGAN FAMILY FARM

James Logan just came in from working in the fields. He kissed his wife and sat down at the kitchen table. Matt's mother was setting the table in preparation for the evening meal, when Matt's sister, Anna, bolted in the back door completely out of breath and shouted, "There's a Union patrol headed up the road!" They all walked out to the front porch as a federal major and his men rode up into the front yard. The major dismounted and walked up onto the porch stating, "My men and I have been assigned to patrol this area, and under the authorization of General Order 9, we will be helping ourselves to whatever supplies you may have here. In addition to that, I have been informed that you and your family may very well be Rebel sympathizers, and as such, we will be inspecting your home to see if you have any firearms. As you know, under martial law, all firearms are to be confiscated."

Matt's father looked at the major with a withering glare and stated: "We have no firearms here, and we barely have enough to feed me and my family."

The major smugly looked at him, waved the soldiers in the front door of the house, and chided him, "You should've thought of that before you turned traitor and started helping those damned guerrillas." The leader turned and told his second-in-command to make camp in the barn lot, slaughter two of the cows, and help themselves to whatever other supplies they could find.

Straightaway, Mrs. Logan went into the house where the soldiers were ransacking all the drawers and cabinets. She followed them upstairs where the soldiers continued their search, and when they pulled open her dresser drawer, they found the gold necklace that Matt's grandmother gave to Matt's mother on her wedding day. The soldier promptly picked up the necklace and put it in his pocket. Matt's mom cried out, "That necklace belonged to my mother, and it is certainly not a weapon!"

The soldier replied," You are very lucky that the major decided, as we rode up here, that we would not drag your husband out and hang him from that tree out front before you and your children." With that, he and the other soldiers turned and headed back downstairs and out to the barn lot to join the others. That night, the family huddled together in fear for their lives.

The next morning, the major walked up to the front porch and knocked on the door. James Logan answered, and the major smiled and stated, "Thank you very much for the hospitality. Seems you had a lot of corn stockpiled and a nice horse and wagon there in the barn. We will be taking that corn, and since we have no way to haul it, we will be taking that horse and wagon as well."

Mr. Logan looked at the man and shouted, "You, sir, are a lowlife, murdering thug, and when you finally meet your maker, you will burn in hell!"

"That may very well be, sir, but I'm sure that you will be there way before I am. Good day!" The major turned, joined his men, mounted up, and gave the order to move out. Matt's dad knew that to have fought the man would be suicide, and he could only stand there and watch as the Union patrol rode off with every-

Matt

thing the Logan family had.

JUNE 26, 1864, COURTHOUSE ROCK (DIARY)

"We traveled so far today about 35 miles over such beautiful hills and rocks. Passed over 60 miles before getting to a ranch at Mud Springs. Are now within 100 miles of Laramie. We got such nice antelope meat for supper tonight. We had bad luck yesterday morning as soon as we started. We started walking and Mr. Hughes mules got spooked by something and took off. When I went to catch them they took fright and ran down the hill and broke the wagon tongue which caused a delay of several hours. We only made about 10 miles and stopped near the Courthouse Rock. Lizzie and I walked up to see it. It was 2 1/2 miles. We were so deceived by the distance. There are hundreds of names cut in the rock but none I knew. It has been so warm today. I presume we will get to Ft. Laramie in two or three more days."

"Two months ago today I left my dear home. I am tonight far away on the banks of the North Platte. How beautiful it is interspersed with those green islands across there. We are near the Chimney Rock though I do not admire it so much as the Courthouse Rock."

INDEPENDENCE, MISSOURI

Bill, Josiah, and the boys swept into town and took the Union post there by surprise. They raced up Spring Street, killing Union guards posted along the route, and headed for the town square and the jail. The guerrillas easily overran the guards and released all the prisoners held there. In the meantime, the main guerrilla force raided the tent camp of the Union forces.

Union Colonel James Buel oversaw of the Union forces in Independence and found himself in a dangerous situation indeed. As the officer in charge, he occupied a residence in the finest hotel in town and set up his headquarters. He now found himself surrounded by the guerrillas who took up positions in the adjacent buildings to open fire on his hotel. He was completely cut off from his men who were under heavy attack at their camp and were disorganized. At 8:30 a.m., Josiah ordered a ceasefire and instructed the men to set fire to the buildings adjoining Buel's headquarters. From behind a couple of barrels across the street, Josiah shouted out to Buel, "Colonel, if you don't surrender, we will roast you alive."

After an hour, Buel's headquarters were sweltering, and he fashioned a white flag out of a bedsheet, stuck it out the window, and called out, "I will surrender provided me and my men are not turned over to Bloody Bill Anderson and executed. We ask that we be treated as prisoners of war."

Josiah called for Bill, and after a lengthy discussion, it was decided that they would allow Buel to surrender provided he and his men lay down their arms, swear an oath they would never take up arms against the Confederacy again, and march to Kansas City. Buel had no choice and accepted the terms. Bill and Archie argued that they should slaughter the entire Union force, but Josiah and the rest of the men convinced them that to do such a thing this close to Kansas City would bring out every Union soldier within 100 miles of Independence.

Buel lost 50 men killed, 120 wounded, and 180 captured. The guerrillas suffered heavy losses as well with 32 killed and 87 wounded, but the men being held in the jail were freed, the town was liberated, and Buel and his men were disarmed and sent packing. In addition, the guerrillas captured 20 wagons of supplies and enough rifles and ammunition to arm them for many months to come.

Josiah was right. The capture of Independence came as a shock to western Missouri. A tremendous guerrilla force appeared out of nowhere and destroyed a major Union post. In Kansas City, the citizens held a town meeting to discuss the protection of the city, and the next day, under the orders of Union General William Rosecrans, rifles were issued, and every able-bodied man was ordered to help defend the community.

JUNE 28, 1864, SCOTT'S BLUFF, NEBRASKA TERRITORY

"We traveled about 25 miles today. Left Chimney Rock and came through Scott's Bluff, the most beautiful place I ever saw, such pretty flowers and cedars. I walked all the way through. We are now in 40 miles from Ft. Laramie. Oh how anxious I am to get there and get letters from home."

"Aunt Sarah, come quick! Johnny Hughes has been bit by a rattlesnake!" cried Matt breathlessly. Sarah asked, "Where is he? You tell him to lay still, and I will get the Hartshorn out of the medicine kit."

"He's up ahead by their wagon, and he doesn't look good," Matt replied. "What is Hartshorn?"

"Hartshorn is a medicine that I prepared for the trip," Sarah answered as she pulled a wooden box out of the wagon. "You make it by boiling down the bones and hooves of the deer we've been eating."

Sarah and Matt ran forward to the Hughes wagon to help Johnny. When they arrived, he was lying on the ground and feeling faint.

Sarah quickly pulled out the jar of medicine, added a small amount to a cup of water, and helped Johnny drink it. She pulled a small knife from the box and made a cut on his leg where he had been bitten. She sucked the poison from the wound and spat it out on the ground. Looking at Johnny's father, she asked, "Mr. Hughes, you have any tobacco?"

"Yes, ma'am, I do," he replied.

"Take some and chop it up so I can make a poultice."

He quickly did so, and Sarah applied it to the wound and wrapped it in cotton cloth.

"Johnny," she said, "you are going to feel terrible for a couple of days, but this should do the trick."

Johnny was so sick, he could only look at Sarah and give her a faint smile of thanks.

Sarah told Mr. Hughes to put Johnny in the wagon and let him ride for a couple of days. Matt and Sarah headed back to their wagon. Sarah stowed the medicine kit, and Matt asked, "Will Johnny be okay?"

Sarah put her hand on Matt's shoulder and said, "He should be, Mattie. We got to him quick. You did the right thing running here to get me."

"Thank goodness you are prepared. You just saved that boy's life."

Sarah said, "This is what Mr. Twitchell has been saying all along. We all need to work together if we are going to make it to California safely. He also told me that since we've stopped, we might as well make camp here, so go get your cousin, and help me make supper."

The day before, Matt and Lizzie hiked to nearby Courthouse Rock. The first travelers on the Oregon Trail named the rock formation because they said it resembled the courthouse in St. Louis. The rock rose to almost 400 feet above the trail. Travelers visited the rock for years and carved their names into the soft stone. Matt and Lizzie did so as well. Lizzie carved the words: "The Logans, West by wagon train, 1864." Matt, on the other hand, was a little more creative and carved a large heart. In the center, she scratched the names: "Matt and Josiah."

That evening at dinner, Mr. Hughes approached and said, "Johnny is doing much better and even asked for something to eat. I can't thank you enough for saving my boy's life."

"It was nothing," Sarah replied, "and I expect you would do the same for me and my family."

Mr. Hughes reached into a sack he was carrying and pulled out a slab of bacon and some hard candy for the girls. "I want you to have this," he said.

Will and Sarah both declared, "There is no need for payment." But Mr. Hughes insisted, saying, "I won't take no for an answer, and besides, since Johnny ain't eatin' much, we have plenty extra." With that, he turned and headed back to his camp.

Sarah looked at the girls, handed them the candy, and noted, "Well, girls, it looks like you get dessert tonight!"

They broke camp and headed out the next morning. Only an hour later, Chimney Rock clearly came into view. Although eight miles in the distance, the rock appeared much closer and was used as a significant landmark by settlers heading west since the 1830s. An Indian legend said that a young brave made the rock, climbed to the top, and fell to his death.

Having traveled all day from their camp at Chimney Rock, the wagon train arrived at the next major landmark, Scotts Bluff.

A story was told that claimed the bluff got its name from Hiram Scott, a mountain man, trapper, and trader from St. Charles, Missouri. Scott was working for William Ashley's Rocky Mountain

Fur Company in 1828, and he and his party were trapping in the area. Scott became deathly ill, and having no medicine, two of his friends put him in their canoe and attempted to take him downstream to seek help. Unfortunately, the boat capsized, and to make matters worse, Scott's leg was broken in the accident. Seeing their friend could travel no further, they decided to leave him on the banks of the river and continue to travel for help.

Winter came early that year, and they were not able to return until the following spring. When they arrived in April at the spot where they left him, there was no sign of Scott. Several months later, another group of trappers found Scott's bones at the base of the bluff. Somehow, he managed to cross the river and drag himself 60 miles to the base of the bluff where they found his body. From that point forward, the rock formation was named Scotts Bluff.

THREE MILES NORTH OF CAPE GIRARDEAU, SCOTT COUNTY, MISSOURI

"We're nearly there. I told you we'd make it, and no one would ever miss us," Union Private Jim Haney said as he turned in his saddle to speak to his buddy, Private Sam Johnson.

Sam replied, "I guess you were right, but this is still the craziest thing we've ever done. If Lieutenant Chapman ever finds out we snuck away from camp there in St. Louis to come all the way down here to see our girlfriends, he could have us shot for being deserters."

Jim laughed, "The Lieutenant couldn't care less where we are. There hasn't been a single thing happen in St. Louis since this war started. With over 4,000 Union troops in St. Louis, they will never know we were missing and would probably be glad to have two fewer soldiers to worry about."

As they crested the hill, they could see Cape Girardeau spread out in the river bottoms below them. Sam asked, "What in the world is that off in the distance south of town?"

"I see it. Looks like the entire Confederate Army is marching this way, "Jim replied. "There has to be over 10,000 of them!"

About that time, an advance patrol of the Confederate forces came into view just below them and spotted the two young men on the ridge. Sam turned to Jim and exclaimed, "The girls are going to have to wait! We need to get the hell out of here!" With that, they turned and rode as fast as they could back in the direction of St. Louis.

After several miles, seeing they weren't being pursued, they slowed their horses, and Sam asked Jim, "What do we do now? Should we go back and file a report as to what we saw? That big a force of Confederate troops is surely headed to St. Louis."

"I agree, but think about this. If we go back and report what we saw, we will have to explain what we were doing way down here when we were supposed to be in St. Louis. If we admit that, they will hang us for sure. As much as I hate to, we simply can't tell them what we saw."

"I knew we wouldn't be able to pull this off," Sam responded. "Now look at the mess we're in. I agree with you. We can't very well tell them what's coming, but we'd best get back there because they're going to need every gun they can get." Spurring their horses, they continued their journey back to St. Louis.

Confederate General Joe Shelby was riding with the advance scouting party that morning and saw the two Union soldiers atop the hill just outside of town. He ordered his men forward and turned to ride back to inform General Sterling Price of the situation. As he approached Price and the rest of the column, he saluted and said, "Sir, we just spotted two Union soldiers on the ridge there above the town. If we were hoping for an element of surprise, I think we can forget that."

Sterling Price returned the salute and, appraising the information, turned to his second-in-command and verbalized his thoughts, "We've been traveling all day, and I was getting ready to make camp anyway. This looks like as good a spot as any. Give the order." Turning to General Shelby, he said, "General, once camp is established, I want you and the other senior officers to meet with me. We need to make a decision."

In the fall of 1864, the Confederate command made final plans to launch a fall raid into Missouri by regular Confederate forces. General Sterling Price, former Governor of Missouri, was to command the invading force, and his objective was to capture St. Louis and, if possible, the entire state. This was the reason why the guerrillas were sent the message to wreak havoc on central Missouri. Their job was to draw forces out of St. Louis and clear the way for General Price's invasion.

It was on September 19, 1864, that General Price entered Missouri with his force of 12,000 Confederate soldiers heading north toward St. Louis and ran into the two Union soldiers just outside Cape Girardeau.

The three, battle-hardened Confederate generals saluted as they stepped into General Price's tent. "Gentlemen, have a seat," said Price upon returning their salute. General Price joined them around a small table in the center of the tent. He looked at the men and thought to himself, "*I could not ask for a better set of commanders*." Seated at the table were General James Fagan, a former Arkansas politician who had proved himself in battle time and again; Major General John S. Marmaduke, a West Point graduate and son of a distinguished Missouri family; and Brigadier General Joseph O. Shelby, a great Cavalry leader and one of the toughest fighters of the war.

"Gentlemen," Price began, "I fear our element of surprise is gone. Those Union scouts will head back to St. Louis and report what they saw. The question before us now is whether we should continue with our original plan of invasion or not."

General Marmaduke was the first to speak. "General Price, as you know, we currently have a force of 12,000 men, but that is all we have. This army was cobbled together with what was left of our forces in Mississippi after the terrible losses we took at Corinth. If the Union forces in St. Louis are forewarned and they bring in additional reinforcements, we could step into a hornet's nest and suffer a defeat from which the Confederacy would not be able to recover."

General Shelby differed, "I don't agree with that. It will take those boys at least two days to get back to St. Louis. If we mount up at first light and push our men, we can attack St. Louis long before reinforcements could arrive."

General Price turned to General Fagan and said, "Well, General, I've heard two sides. What is your opinion?" General Fagan, always the politician, replied, "General, both arguments are valid, but the decision is ultimately yours. I will comply with whatever decision you make."

Price sat silently for several minutes and finally concluded, "I am going to have to side with General Marmaduke; the loss of this army here in Missouri would be a devastating blow to the Confederacy. However, we have a duty to continue our campaign here in our home state. At first light, we will break camp and head for the capital, Jefferson City. If we capture the capital, I am sure the citizens of Missouri, having suffered the abuses of the Union Army, will all rally behind us. We will use Jefferson City as a command headquarters, shut down river traffic, resupply our army, and recruit a force of Missouri citizens to launch an overwhelming attack on St. Louis in the spring."

The next morning, the Confederates broke camp and headed westward toward the capital. Six days later, as the Confederate forces continued on their trek toward Jefferson City, a scout from General Marmaduke's forward patrol approached the main army and reported to General Price. "General Marmaduke sends his compliments and asks me to inform you that less than a day's ride from your current position is a Union fort at Pilot Knob. The General respectfully requests that you advance the main force with all haste to attack the fort."

General Price replied, "Is that so, Lieutenant? Since when was General Marmaduke put in command of this operation? " The lieutenant, with fear in his eyes, replied, "Sir, General Marmaduke told me to expect such a reply and to inform you that none other than General Thomas Ewing is manning Union Fort Davidson with a force of just 900 men."

"Are you sure he said Thomas Ewing?" Price responded.

"Yes, sir, the same Union general that issued General Order Number 11 and forced my family out of their home in Jackson County."

The former governor turned in his saddle, looked at Generals Fagan and Shelby, and said, "Boys, Thomas Ewing is the most hated man in this state. I think a little detour is in order." He then turned to the Lieutenant and said, "Report back to General Marmaduke, and tell him we're headed his way." The lieutenant saluted, turned his horse, and headed off down the road.

General Thomas Ewing previously was the commander of the District of the Border headquartered in Kansas City. It was during his time there that Quantrill organized a force of 200 guerrillas and conducted a raid on the town of Lawrence, Kansas. Quantrill gave the order as they rode into town to kill every man old enough to carry a gun. The guerrillas carried out that order with ferocity, killing boys as young as eight and men as old as 80. When they finished, they set fire to the town and burned it to the ground. After their work was done, they rode back to Missouri.

Senator Jim Lane, who organized the Jayhawks, lived in Lawrence. He escaped from being killed by running from his home into a cornfield, where Lane hid until the raid was over. When he came out of hiding and saw his house burning and the devastation to his town, he mounted his horse and headed to Kansas City. When he arrived, he went straight to Union Headquarters and confronted General Ewing.

"I would like to know just what the hell you and your men have been doing to hunt down and exterminate these outlaws who are wreaking havoc on the citizens of Kansas!" Senator Lane shouted.

Ewing looked at him and answered, "Senator, I know you are upset, but I don't appreciate the tone of your voice. I've stationed troops up and down the entire border, and every waking minute, I am committing additional forces to bring them to justice."

Jim Lane was shaking with rage and roared at the general: "That, sir, is not good enough. Perhaps you have forgotten how much influence I have in Washington. If I have my way, you will lose your command position here and be transferred to a position manning some fort in the middle of nowhere. However, before I leave this office today, you will issue this General Order." Senator Lane reached into his vest pocket and pulled out a paper which he handed to General Ewing.

Thomas Ewing knew this was no idle threat. He took the paper, read it, and called his aide into the room. "Lieutenant!" he barked, as he handed the paper to his subordinate, who scurried into the room, "Take this and draft it up in formal form as a General Order. I want this issued no later than tomorrow morning." The lieutenant saluted and left the room. General Ewing turned to Senator Lane and said, "You realize this will bring down a firestorm upon us." The senator, still shaking with rage, snapped, "General, I couldn't care less what happens to you and your career. These raids into Kansas will stop, and they will stop right now!" He turned and stormed out of the office.

The next day, General Order Number 11 was issued. It stated: "All Missourians living in Jackson, Cass, Bates, and the northern half of Vernon counties shall be removed. You will vacate the area within 15 days or be shot on sight by order of General Thomas Ewing."

To make matters worse, General Ewing selected Jennison's Jayhawkers to carry out the order. The revenge-seeking Jayhawkers burned every building including houses, barns, and storage sheds after they carted off all the food, livestock, and personal possessions of the citizens being banished. Murdering and robbing their way south from Kansas City, all four counties who suffered at the hands of the Jayhawks were from that point forward referred to as "the burnt district."

Pilot Knob, Missouri

As General Price and his army approached the ridge just south of Fort Davidson, General Marmaduke rode up and reported, "Sir, it looks like we will have the element of surprise. General Ewing and his men are in the fort, and except for a few men stationed on the guard towers, it looks like they're all settled in for the close of the day and their evening meal."

Price quickly surveyed the situation. The fort, surrounded by a six-foot-high berm of dirt, stood in a small valley surrounded by hills in the Iron Mountain range. It was a foolish place to build a fort. Any opposing force with artillery could take up positions on the surrounding hills and bomb the fort into submission. General Price knew this and saw the opportunity, but daylight was fading fast. By the time he could get the artillery into position, it would be too late to launch an attack. He turned to his generals and instructed them, "Men, the smart thing to do would be to surround this place with our big guns and open fire, but I fear we would have to wait until tomorrow morning to do so. With 12,000 men versus their 900, I would suggest we take advantage of the element of surprise and attack immediately. General Fagan, you approach from the north. General Marmaduke the west. General Shelby, you and I will take the remainder of the forces and attack from the south."

The men rapidly moved their troops into position, and the signal was given to attack. All 12,000 men let out blood-curdling Rebel yells and charged forward. They quickly reached the dirt berm surrounding the fort, only to find that the dirt had been excavated from a ditch on the backside of the berm between them and the fort. As the men crested the ridge and slid into the ditch, the Union forces opened fire. It was a bloodbath. In less than 20 minutes, the Confederates suffered nearly 2,000 casualties. Price saw the calamity and immediately ordered a retreat.

The Confederates took up positions out of rifle range in the valley surrounding the fort awaiting further orders. Price called his generals together and repented. "Men this was my fault. In my rush to take Ewing, I ignored the right strategy and got a lot of my boys killed."

Joe Shelby tried to console him. "General," he declared softly, "there was no way to know that a ditch full of mud and water was on the other side of that dirt berm. I've never seen that in any other fort we've ever attacked, but I will sure remember it next time we're trying to hold a fort of our own."

"We took a beating today, but it will not happen tomorrow," the silver-haired commander replied. "Tell the men to make camp surrounding the fort. General Fagan, while the rest of the men are making camp and tending to the wounded, I want you to take your artillery units and place them on those ridges over there. At first light, we're going to do this the right way and bomb that fort into oblivion."

Inside the fort, General Thomas Ewing gathered his officers together. "Men," he stated, "you fought well today, and I'm proud of all of you. However, we now find ourselves surrounded by a huge force. It appears that the Confederates are moving their artillery into positions on the surrounding ridges. Unless we can figure a way out of here, they will open fire at first light. We won't stand a chance."

"What do you suggest, sir?" inquired one of his officers. "Shall we ask for terms?"

Ewing looked at the young man and explained, "After the whooping you men put on those Rebels today, I don't think they plan on giving us any acceptable terms. That leaves us with two choices. We can stay here and fight to the death or try to escape. I for one do not plan on dying in this godforsaken place, and I have a plan."

General Ewing told his officers to have everyone change out of their uniforms and into their civilian clothes, including them. Once this was done, he assembled the entire force on the parade ground in the center of the fort. There he explained his plan. Under cover of darkness, the men were to pair up, and at various points along the line, two soldiers should slip out every 10 minutes and walk casually through the Rebel camp. General Ewing stressed to the men that it was of the utmost importance that none of them break and run. Dressed in civilian clothes, they looked just like any of the Rebel forces surrounding them. He told the men to take their time, stopping occasionally. Once they made their way through the Rebel camp, they were to all meet up two miles east of camp on the road heading back to St. Louis.

At about 10 p.m., the first soldier slipped out, and for the remainder of the evening, additional soldiers followed. At the break of dawn, the last two soldiers lit a long fuse running to the powder magazine and then slipped out as well. At first light, an immense explosion rocked the valley, and timbers from the fort flew in every direction. The Rebels quickly jumped up, grabbed their rifles, and watched the fort burn.

As the flames died down later that morning, General Price and his men rode into the fort only to find that Ewing and all his men indeed escaped. General Price turned in his saddle and told his officers, "We should have never stopped here. Break camp and prepare to move out for Jefferson City. We leave in one hour. I certainly hope that our guerrilla friends up north are having better luck than we have."

JULY 3, 1864, FORT LARAMIE (DIARY)

"One year ago today I was in Ralls County, Missouri, at a Catholic wedding and had such a nice time. How strange that I am now so far away. We got to Fort Laramie this afternoon. Laramie is a very pretty place on the Laramie River. The Union flag was waving there and plenty of Federal soldiers, so Mr. Twitchell decided we should pass on through and make camp about 6 miles west of the fort. He was afraid that some of the men with us may not be able to keep their mouths shut about where their sympathies lay if asked about the war. The last thing we need is more problems with the Union way out here in the middle of nowhere. After we made camp we did a good days washing and then went after wild gooseberries and made a pie for supper. Also made a vinegar pie. All ate heartily of course."

Fort Laramie was named for Jacques La Ramee', a French-Canadian trapper who operated in the early 1800s in the territory which is now Wyoming. He was killed by Arapaho Indians in 1820. The fort was unique in that it was built of bricks dried in the sun. Blockhouses stood at each corner where the walls were about 15 feet high and topped with guard towers. Fort Laramie was where Lakota Sioux War Chief Red Cloud made his famous speech: "We will fight you every mile of the way to the Big Horn. We will let your milestones be the graves of your dead. You have lied to us and have now nothing to expect of us but War! War! War!"

July 11, 1864, Devils Gate (Diary)

"We've been traveling all day in the Black Hills. I've never seen anything more beautiful all covered with cedars and pines. The roads were rough. We traveled through Devils Gate and are now in camp in full view of it. The scenery here is beautiful. Lizzie and I went up there this evening after 10. Had company. Mr. Higgins went with Lizzie and Mr. Wade went with me. I enjoyed the scene very much. So grand I can never forget it, though after we were gone, some of the folks here made remarks about our company. But I am not caring for what they say. The Sweetwater River runs through the Devils Gate. So clear and pretty and so many rocks. Mr. Wade told us when we arrived there it is 330 feet deep and only 30 feet wide and that it would make a good ambush spot for Indians, which scared Lizzie and I to death. But even more frightful was the story he told us about four girls who were here last year and climbed to the top. One poor girl lost her footing and fell to her death. He said her tombstone read:

Here lies the body of Carolyn Todd,

Whose soul has lately gone to God,

Ere redemption was too late,

She was redeemed at Devils Gate!

Needless to say, we were very careful where we stepped as we made our way back to camp that night."

July 22, 1864, Fort Bridger (Diary)

"We passed through Fort Bridger this morning. It is a very pretty place on the Blacks Fork River. The country now is beautiful with such grand hills and cedars and flowers. I had the good luck to get two letters there.

One from Kate Clarke [Quantrill]. In her letter, Kate said that Josiah and the boys are still operating in central Missouri and are well. She also informed me that mother and father had a run in with the Union and although the Union soldiers robbed them, they, and my brother and sisters, were left unharmed. Oh how I hope that this did not happen because of my relationship with Josiah. If he hears of this, I fear he will subject himself to undue risk to exact his revenge upon the Provost Marshal and his men."

Fort Bridger was first established in 1843 as a trading post by a mountain man, Jim Bridger, at the junction of the Blacks Fork and Green rivers. He traded with the local Indians and emigrants traveling west on the Oregon Trail. During his previous years, Bridger journeyed throughout the area as a fur trapper and was the first white man to see the Great Salt Lake. Fort Bridger, unlike Fort Laramie, was nothing more than a crude trading post, but it did have all the necessary supplies for the wagon trains to continue their journey westward.

SINGLETON FARM, 3 MILES EAST OF CENTRALIA, MISSOURI

Josiah and Bloody Bill heard that Confederate Colonel David Poole, who had been sent into the state by the Confederacy to recruit men to the cause, and Captain George Todd, who had previously ridden with Quantrill, were camped with their forces on the farm of Colonel M. G. Singleton, an ex-Confederate officer at home on parole and under bond. They headed in that direction, and when they arrived, they found the guerrilla camp was perfect. On all sides of the camp, there was a long stretch of prairie; there was no way Union patrols could sneak up on them without being seen.

As they moved into camp, Bill and his men were immediately recognized and told the officers were headquartered in the barn. Riding forward, they dismounted and were met by Colonel Singleton. "Bill," joked Singleton, "I can't believe they haven't caught up with you, yet. You have wreaked havoc in this area, and every Union soldier within 100 miles of here is hunting for you."

"Colonel, it's great to see you," responded Bill. "I heard you'd been killed down at Corinth." The colonel smiled and said, "Well, they thought they got me, but as you can see, I'm still here. Truth is, I took a round in the shoulder, and with the help of friends, I was able to make it back home. The wife and daughter did a great job patching me up. Unfortunately, things got so bad around here that the girls insisted I stay and not go back south. So, I marched down to the local courthouse, signed an oath of loyalty to the Union, and posted a thousand-dollar bond. I can't believe those Yankees would ever think that I would give up my support of the South, but I guess they just don't know any better. You and your boys are welcome here. Help yourself to whatever supplies you need. George and David are in the barn. I'm sure they'll be glad to see you."

Anderson turned to Josiah and said, "Take the men and head on down there to that stand of trees and make camp. I'll be along shortly." Josiah turned and headed off in that direction.

Bill entered the barn. George and David immediately looked up, and David declared, "As I live and breathe, there's the ghost that everyone has been talking about."

Bill smiled, and George exclaimed, "Bill, you've been a busy man! When Jeff Davis said to create a diversion, you didn't mess around."

The guerrilla leader grinned and replied, "Well, I've been doing the best I can with the small force I have. How many men do you guys have here? It looks like an army."

George responded, "John Thrailkill just showed up this morning with over 100 men. He's been recruiting up to the northwest of here. David showed up with nearly 150 men. So, all told, I'd say we have around 300 to 350 men."

"What do you plan to do with all these men?"

"Our orders were to recruit as many men as possible and get them south across the Missouri River to join up with Price's forces," David answered. "I expect we will be heading out the day after tomorrow."

Bloody Bill just shook his head and said, "I wish you boys luck; as for me, my orders are to continue stirring the pot up here. I'm worn out. If you don't mind, I'll take my leave and go join my boys."

George and David nodded in agreement, and David said, "Happy hunting, Bill, until we meet again."

The next morning, Bill woke up early, kicked Josiah in his bedroll, and said, "Josiah, get your ass up. We're headed to town to get the paper. I want to see what they have to say about what we've been doing here in central Missouri. Get the rest of the boys up." Josiah rubbed the sleep out of his eyes, stretched, and roused the rest of their squad. The others in the camp were still sound asleep, but Anderson and his men were used to getting up at the crack of dawn. They quickly mounted up and headed for Centralia.

Centralia was a small railroad town with a population of only 100 people, and they were all sound asleep when Bill and the boys rode into town firing their guns and shouting the Rebel yell, terrorizing the citizens as they jumped from their beds. The men hit the bar first and helped themselves to all the whiskey they could carry. Then they went door to door robbing the citizens systematically. About noon, the westbound North Central Missouri train from St. Charles whistled in the distance, and Bill and the men quickly piled railroad ties on the tracks and hid in the nearby buildings. As the train pulled up and slowed to a stop, it was surrounded by the guerrillas. Bill and his men boarded the train.

"Boys, I want you to rob every passenger on this train except those men who have calluses on their hands. Those men are hardworking citizens, and I will not rob them. Everyone else is fair game." As they made their way from car to car, they entered a car which held 25 unarmed Union soldiers. Bill stepped into the car and told Archie, "March these men down to the loading platform." Archie did as ordered.

Once on the platform, the Union soldiers were told to strip out of their clothes because the guerrillas needed their uniforms. Bill stepped off the train and instructed Archie to march the men across the street and line them up against the brick wall of the bank. Archie did so, and Bill gave the order to: "Muster-out these men." Archie and the rest of the guerrillas turned and opened fire on the men, killing all except one of the soldiers who ran wounded and crawled under the wooden train platform. The guerrillas set fire to the station and the platform; when the man ran out, they finished him.

The train was set on fire without anyone aboard and sent off in the direction of Sturgeon, Missouri. Bill smiled and remarked, "Boys, we got our newspaper. Looks like our work is done here. Mount up, and let's head back to camp." The men straddled their horses and headed back to Singleton's farm.

About four that afternoon, Union Major Johnson and his infantry unit from Paris, Missouri, rode into Centralia and found the town in a state of shock. Hearing there were only 30 guerrillas in the band who did all this damage, Johnson divided his command and left half of his men in town, while he and the other half rode out after the guerrillas.

A mile out of town, Major Johnson saw 10 horsemen ahead of them who retreated down the road. He set off in immediate pursuit. Little did Johnson know that the horsemen were doing exactly as they were told, and Johnson led his men straight into an ambush. As he neared the Singleton farm, he crested the hill and saw nearly 300 mounted guerrillas waiting for them. Seeing he couldn't retreat, Johnson, in a true act of bravery, dismounted his men and formed a 20-yard line of battle.

Bill saw this, turned in his saddle, and shouted, "These boys are crazy. Charge!"

Major Johnson gave the order to his men, "Hold your fire until they are close." When the guerrillas were within 50 yards, Johnson gave the order to fire. Unfortunately, shooting downhill, the infantry fired their volley, but most of the rounds went high. Only three guerrillas fell. In a matter of seconds, the Rebels were on the Union troops, and in no time, the Yankees were wiped out. Major Johnson himself, firing his pistol, was shot down by 17-year-old Jesse James.

The guerrillas raced back into Centralia and finished off the rest of Johnson's men. Only nine of Johnson's original force of 158 men were able to retreat to Paris. The guerrillas turned and rode back to Singleton's farm, and Bill gave the order to finish off any of the wounded.

Wiping out this massive Union force threw panic into the hearts of all the people of Central Missouri. Anderson and his men accomplished their mission.

July 28, 1864, Salt Lake City (Diary)

"We arrived about noon today. I have not seen much of the city. From all appearances I do not think it is as grand a place as I had expected. I think it is a fine place to get good eatables as there have been Mormon women every moment since our arrival with vegetables and fruit for sale. We have plenty of onions and beef steak for supper. I had one letter from home. Great troubles in Missouri. I wonder what will be her fate, poor downtrodden state. I pray Josiah and my family are safe. The weather is very warm now. I have suffered very much with heat in the last day or two. This place has a great many shade trees."

JULY 29, 1864, SALT LAKE CITY (DIARY)

"*I walked around today to see Brigham Young's residence. Also the foundation of the Temple which was very grand though it will not be finished in our day. Altogether I think this is a very nice city. I went to hear Brigham Young, the President of Utah, preach this evening. He speaks well and is a very fine-looking man. They had good singing by the choir and there were some good-looking ladies there. I wonder what he would say if he knew I was from Missouri where our Governor issued an extermination order for all Mormons living there? Thankfully this is our last day in Salt Lake I think as we are expecting to start out tomorrow and go a few miles to grass. The weather is still warm and sultry. I am weary. Oh God watch over me and protect me from the snares of this sinful world.*"

Mormons once held a stronghold in the state of Missouri when their leader, Joseph Smith, pronounced Independence, Missouri, as the location of Zion in 1831. In their religion, Independence was to be the New Jerusalem where followers would gather for the second coming of Christ. Missourians didn't like the abolitionist views and polygamy practices of the Mormon settlers, and it provoked what became known as the Mormon War.

The people of Boonville, Missouri, led the charge to rid the state of all Mormons and sent a delegation to Jefferson City to gain support from the governor and the state legislature. Hearing the testimony of the people of Boonville, Governor Lilburn Boggs issued Executive Order 44, "The Extermination Order," on October 27, 1838. It declared the Mormons must be treated as enemies and must be exterminated or driven from the state.

Governor Boggs, having signed the order, dispatched the State Militia, who attacked the Mormons at Hans Mill, Missouri. The Mormons suffered many casualties and fled east, led by Joseph Smith, to Nauvoo, Illinois. There, Joseph Smith rebuilt his following. His numbers quickly reached several thousand, and the congregation went to work building a new temple in which to worship.

Just as was the case in Missouri, word spread rapidly to the surrounding communities about Joseph Smith, his followers, and their beliefs. Local papers reported that, in addition to Smith considering himself a king and forming his own private army of 5,000 men, he was practicing polygamy and had eight wives. This was more than the local community could bear. A warrant was issued for his arrest. On June 25, 1844, Joseph and his brother Hyrum, surrendered to the local Sheriff in nearby Carthage, Illinois. They were placed in the Carthage jail to await trial.

Before a jury could be formed, a mob of about 200 armed men from the town stormed the jailhouse. Seeing the size of the crowd, the jailers stepped aside, and the group entered the jail where they shot and killed Joseph Smith and his brother in their cell. The next day, hearing of the death of their leader, panic set in among the members of the Mormon community in Nauvoo. At this point, Brigham Young stepped into the role of Mormon leader.

Seeing that to remain in Illinois would be suicide, he made the decision to pack up lock, stock, and barrel and lead the congregation westward to Salt Lake City where they set up a new Mormon state known as Deseret. Matt and the wagon train arrived in this very community — a society over which Brigham Young exercised complete control, not only over the church but also all civil activities.

August 9, 1864, Tuesday, Indian Springs (Diary)

"Left Salt Lake City four days ago and passed the Great Salt Lake. It was a grand site [sight], so clear and beautiful. We are camping in a very pretty place in a canyon. Had one of the most awful hills to come down I ever saw. This place is called Indian Springs and has the coldest, best water I ever drank. There are a good many here getting rested and ready for the 40 mile desert. I hope we get through safely. One of our men, Hugh Todd, went out to look for mules that were missing and he was either thrown from his mule or murdered by Indians. He has never been heard of since his mule came to camp without him."

"Matt, you need to run down to the creek and get your aunt and Lizzie," Will instructed. "Mr. Twitchell has called a meeting and wants to talk to everybody." Matt did as she was told, and shortly after that, all the families in the wagon train gathered around the campfire next to Twitchell's wagon.

"Ladies and gentlemen, as you all know, we set out to cross the 40-mile desert tomorrow," the wagon master said. "I've called you together to tell you what to expect and how to prepare. First, I'm sure you've all heard that we will be following the Humboldt River. The truth is, it used to be a river. While there is some water, it is barely drinkable, and most of the time, the river is bone dry. We've been on the trail for three months now. I know our animals are weak, and our wagons are showing many signs of wear and tear, but unfortunately, the worst is yet to come."

He went on to explain, "I was through here a year ago, and one of my men counted over 1,000 graves along the trail through the desert. Thousands of animals died out there as well. Adding to our problems, the Indians out here have absolutely nothing and are starving to death. For that reason, we will double the guards at night to protect our livestock."

"Second, you need to get rid of everything that is not absolutely necessary. The only things you should be hauling in your wagons are food, water, and the basic necessities."

Several of the women could be heard to gasp. Mrs. Johnson was the first to speak up, "Does this mean I have to get rid of my mother's pipe organ? She brought it here all the way from Scotland and gave it to me as a wedding present!"

Mrs. Burns followed, "What about my china? It, too, is a family heirloom."

Twitchell replied, "Ladies, you have a choice to make. Would you rather have your children die of thirst in the middle of the desert or keep your pipe organ and your china?"

Mrs. Johnson looked at her husband defiantly and said, "Well, if I have to give up Mother's pipe organ, we are certainly not going to carry that stupid iron anvil any further on the trail."

Mr. Johnson replied, "That stupid anvil will come in handy once we make it to California, and I can open up my blacksmith shop."

The wagon master gave Mr. Johnson an evil stare and said, "Do you mean to tell me you've been hauling an anvil in that wagon all this way? It is no wonder your team is worn out. That anvil stays here. As for the rest, you men, just like the women, need to get rid of everything in that wagon that you can't eat or drink. The one exception I'll make is your weapons. We may very well need them."

"Now, the final item," Mr. Twitchell continued. "We will leave here tomorrow night at sunset, and throughout the journey, until we reach the mountains, we will be traveling at night. The temperatures during the day are way too hot for people or livestock to tolerate. Every day we'll set out at dusk and travel till sunrise. We will then circle the wagons as we always have and make camp, sleeping under the wagons during the day to protect us from the sun. If there aren't any further questions, I suggest you all get a good night's rest, clean out those wagons first thing tomorrow morning, and spend the afternoon filling every pot, pan, water vessel, and barrel you have with water from the spring." With no further questions, everyone headed back to their respective wagons.

The next morning, Will, Sarah, Lizzie, and Matt went through the wagon, discarding most of their possessions. "Mother," asked Lizzie, "Do Matt and I have to give up our trunk with all of our pretty dresses and shoes? What about the china?"

Sarah looked tearfully at Lizzie and said, "I'm sorry, Lizzie, I thought we could take these things with us all the way to California, but I was wrong. Your lives are a lot more important than any dress, and I promise, as soon as we get to California, I will take you both shopping and buy each of you two new dresses."

"I don't know what you girls are complaining about," Will complained, "I had 10 stone crocs of the finest Missouri whiskey, and I had to pour it out and refill them with spring water!"

His wife and the girls couldn't help but break out laughing, and Sarah said, "Well, it looks like each one of us is having to sacrifice."

Matt asked her uncle, "I saw Mr. and Mrs. Johnson dig a hole and bury that pipe organ and anvil. Why in the world would they do that?"

Will smiled and explained, "Well, Matt, some of these fools actually think they'll be back through here one day, and they'll pick up that stuff. Some have even gone to the trouble of marking the burial site as a grave, thinking no one will mess with it. Truth is, those Mormons back in Salt Lake have groups of men with wagons who set out east and west on the trail every week for the sole purpose of picking up all the treasures left behind. They are onto that trick of disguising the burial site as a grave, and that's the first place they look when they come across one. The Mormons have no way to manufacture anything. Where do you think they got all that stuff they were selling at their market?"

Matt couldn't believe what she just heard and exclaimed, "Good grief! Isn't that stealing? I thought they were people of God." Her uncle just smiled and answered, "I reckon once you lay stuff at the side of the road, it is no longer yours and belongs to the first person who finds it. We'd best get back to work."

That night at dusk, the wagon train set out across the desert.

STERLING PRICE'S CONFEDERATE CAMP, 3 MILES SOUTHEAST OF JEFFERSON CITY, MISSOURI

Having suffered a humiliating defeat at Pilot Knob, General Sterling Price and his army made their way to Jefferson City, where they made camp and sent out scouts to survey the situation in town.

"General, the scouts have returned with their reports," General Marmaduke declared as he approached General Price, who was sitting by a campfire with Generals Shelby and Fagan.

"Very well," Price said. "Let's have it."

Marmaduke sat on the log next to General Fagan and reported, "Well, sir, the news is not good. Although we outnumber the Union forces two to one, they have 4,000 men who are dug into fortified positions on all the high ground surrounding the city. We counted four fortresses all armed with heavy artillery that can reach out and produce a crossfire on troops approaching from any direction. In addition, two of those forts can also fire on the river. The problem is, these men have been there for three years with nothing to do but fortify this city. The capital can be taken, but it will be at a tremendous cost."

After a lengthy discussion among the officers hashing out possible tactics, General Price finally concluded, "Men, I've listened to all our possible options, but with each and every choice, we are looking at losing at least 50% of our forces. I fear that, even if we are successful, what will be left of our army will not be enough to hold the capital. No reinforcements will come to save us. Our best option at this point is to bypass the capital and head to Boonville, a town we know we can trust, and meet up with the guerrillas who have been operating in that area and having great success. The decision has been made. The capital will be spared. We break camp and head for Boonville at first light."

FORTY-MILE DESERT

As they continued their trek across the 40-mile desert by the light of the moon, they came upon an abandoned wagon. The canvas covering was rotted away, and the team pulling the wagon was nothing more than bleached bones in the sand. A short distance farther, they came upon what appeared to be the family belonging to the wagon. Alongside the road were three skeletons, apparently those of a father, mother, and small child.

"Oh! How horrible! What do you suppose happened?" asked Lizzie.

Sarah turned her gaze away from the scene and replied, "That poor family obviously succumbed to the heat. I would imagine that when their team gave out, they grabbed what they could from their wagon and tried to make it on foot. They either ran out of water or simply panicked and tried to move forward in the heat of the day."

"Should we not stop and give them a proper burial?" Matt asked.

"I only wish we could," her aunt responded, "but as Mr. Twitchell said, we must keep moving forward, or we will suffer the same fate. Fear not. I am sure these poor souls are now in the hands of God."

They continued in silence and at first light circled the wagons and made camp next to boiling hot springs flowing out of the dry Humboldt Riverbed. As Lizzie and Matt approached the springs, Will called out, "You girls take care near that water! It is boiling hot and will scald you if you happen to fall in!"

"How can that be?" asked Lizzie.

"I don't rightly know," Will replied. "Everything else is hot here, so I guess that's just the way the water is as well."

"Can we fill your jugs?" asked Matt.

Uncle Will replied, "I wish we could, but that water is filled with salt, and it'll kill the livestock if they drink it, and although it wouldn't kill us, it ain't fit to drink. I suppose you could use it for cooking if you had to, but I think we have enough water to get us through, so I'd steer clear of it."

About that time, a small dog wandered up to the spring. As it leaned down to get a drink, it lost its footing and fell in. It let out a yelp, and the girls desperately tried to grab the poor animal to save it. Will ran forward when he heard the girls scream and quickly grabbed a pitchfork to try to fish the dog out of the water. Just out of their reach, they all stood helplessly and watched the dog boil alive. With the girls in tears, Will led them back to camp.

About an hour later, after the girls calmed down, Mr. Twitchell came to their camp and asked how their water supply was holding out. Will replied, "Provided tomorrow is no worse than today, we should be okay. We have two barrels of water left, and I've only used about one-quarter of the grass we stockpiled in the wagon for the team. They don't eat much in this relentless heat."

"That's good," Mr. Twitchell allowed. "The rest of the train seems to be in about the same shape, and we are over halfway across the desert." He smiled. "We should make Willow Springs by first light tomorrow. There, we will have access to fresh water and additional supplies if you need them. It is also a telegraph office.

We will sleep under the wagons through the heat of the day today and leave again this evening as the sun sets. We no longer have to worry about Indians or wild animals out here. Our greatest enemy right now is the sun and lack of water. I would caution you, however, that as you awake and make plans for setting out this evening, you shake out your bedrolls and boots to make sure there are no scorpions or rattlesnakes that have taken up residence there. They, too, will seek shade here in camp while you sleep."

"Oh, my!" exclaimed Matt. "How will I ever be able to sleep now?"

"Don't worry, Matt," Will assured her. "I'll keep an eye out. You'll be safe. Now get some rest."

Regardless of Will's word, Matt and Lizzie slept most of the night with one eye open, just in case.

That night they set out again.

August 13, 1864, Saturday Willow Springs (Diary)

"In camp here at the telegraph station. Traveled all night. The night, under a full moon, was light and beautiful. We have come 25 miles and got here in time for breakfast. There are a good many campers here. The water is very good. There are such deep holes of water. One mule got into one today and came very near getting killed. I am feeling so lonely and have not written in a while, so I wrote a note home to Josiah. The man at the telegraph station assured me that my letter would be included in the next batch of mail he sent out."

"Dearest Josiah,

James Michael Pasley

> *I commenced writing the other day as we set out on our journey across the desert. Since then we have come 100 miles and have traveled three nights. It was the hottest I have ever been, but the moon shone bright. We had a very high mountain of sand to walk up in which we sank up to our ankles. This was the great desert you have heard so often about. They say this is the most difficult part of the journey and I certainly believe them. I have never been so tired and thirsty. I have seen things here in the desert that will haunt me for the rest of my life and I thank God that we survived. The telegraph operator lives here all by himself. I do not know how he does it. Fortunately, he is a good rebel and took a liking to our group. He joined us in camp this evening and played well on the guitar, singing many familiar rebel songs. You would have really enjoyed it.*
>
>> *I pray you are all right. Way out here we get no news. I have not heard from mother and father and if you are in their area could you please go by and check on them. I know they would love to see you, Bill, and the boys again and you know that they will provide you with anything you need to continue the resistance. If you find them well, please write and let me know. We will be leaving here shortly and following the Truckee River making our way eventually to Carson City where we will enter the mountains. I understand there is a post office. Please send any news you have there. Please be careful. Keep me in your thoughts and prayers as I do you.*
>
> Love,
>
> Matt"

BOONVILLE MISSOURI, OCTOBER 1864

Bloody Bill, Josiah, and the boys rode into Boonville. Josiah turned to Anderson and said, "Ain't this a helluva note? Three years after this war started, we wind up right back where we began. I was here with General Price at the Battle of Boonville. Wasn't much of a battle, just a bunch of Missouri farm boys up against 3,000 Union soldiers out of St. Louis. Best we could do was fight a running rear guard action and escape with our lives."

Bill looked at Josiah and said, "Way I hear it, you boys fought well and put the fear of God in that Captain Nathaniel Lyon, who was leading those Union boys. I understand not long after that, you led them all the way down to Springfield and gave them a proper whoopin' at Wilson's Creek."

Josiah smiled and replied, "That was a great day for the Confederacy. We even killed that pompous ass Nathaniel Lyon, who had been promoted to general, of all things, based on that little skirmish in Boonville.

The group rode down Main Street and dismounted at the hotel where General Price made his headquarters. Bloody Bill led the way, and upon entering the lobby, they spotted General Price seated at a table surrounded by his staff. The general looked up from the orders he was signing, and remarked, "I sure am glad to see you boys. We've had a terrible string of bad luck, and a big part of it has been the fact that these boys riding with me don't know Missouri the way you do." Several of the officers on Price's staff glared at Anderson and his men after hearing this comment.

The partisan leader responded, "Well, General, it's boys like Josiah here who have been born and raised in these parts, who have made our guerrilla campaign so successful. Seems like wherever we go, one of my men has been there, knows the lay of the land, and knows folks who will help us along the way."

Price dismissed his staff and told Bill, Josiah, and the rest of the guerrillas to pull up a chair. He told his aide to fetch two bottles of the best whiskey in the house and glasses for all of them. When the whiskey arrived, General Price and the guerrillas each poured three fingers, and Price proposed a toast, "There are good ships and wood ships and ships that sail the seas, but the best ships are friendships, may they always be!" Everyone drank up and refilled their glasses.

The general got down to business. "Gentlemen," he said, "I entered the state with 12,000 men, and I am now down to less than 3,000. I have not had any reports from our southern headquarters in over a month. Although I was unable to capture St. Louis, I do plan to wreak havoc on the Union forces occupying this state. This is my home. I am a former governor of Missouri, and I will not rest until every one of these Union invaders is driven from our soil. The only way I can do that is with your help."

Josiah spoke up. "General, I was here with your forces when they formed as the Missouri Guard under Governor Claiborne Fox Jackson. I fought for you during the Battle of Boonville, Wilson's Creek, Pea Ridge, and even at Lexington, before I decided to join up with the guerrillas. It would be an honor to serve under your command again, sir."

Price looked at Josiah and responded, "Well, first thing, son, thank you for your service. After that battle at Lexington, we had 40,000 Union troops dispatched out of Kansas City and St. Louis looking for us. We had no choice but to leave the state back in '61, but I know a lot of you men showed true bravery by staying behind and continuing the war through your guerrilla campaigns. It is I who am honored to serve in your ranks."

"General, exactly what is it you want us to do?" Anderson wanted to know.

Sterling Price turned to him and said, "I need to divide up my troops, and I ask you to do the same by assigning one or two of your guerrillas to each of my units."

"General, just like Josiah, it would be an honor to work with you and your men. What's the plan?"

After a lengthy meeting, each of the guerrillas walked out of the hotel with their new missions. Bill and Josiah were assigned to General Joe Shelby's camp, and they were ordered to head north and destroy the Northern Missouri railroad. The James boys were given the task of heading south of Boonville to destroy the Pacific Railroad. The Younger brothers were sent east to attack Union outposts at Danville, New Florence, and High Hill.

The next morning, Anderson, Josiah, and little Archie led General Shelby's men north to the city of Glasgow. Bill, being in charge, made assignments to the men as they stopped at a high ridge overlooking the town. "General Shelby, if you look just to the south of that grain silo, you can make out the railroad depot. It is only manned by four union troops and a telegraph officer. Just to the east of town is a 200-foot-long railroad bridge made of heavy timber. The Union has a force of 50 men encamped on this side of the river, whose sole job is to protect that bridge. I will leave it up to you to determine your plan of attack on the depot and the bridge. Me and my men will attack the river crossing on the main road about a mile north of town."

"General Price was right," Shelby remarked. "You boys know this country like the back of your hand and know more about Union troop movements than Union commanders headquartered in St. Louis! Good hunting. We will meet you back at Boonville."

"Good hunting to you, sir," Bill Anderson replied as General Shelby and his men rode off.

Josiah turned to Bill, "Are you crazy? Why would we ride north to the river crossing? There is nothing there."

The Captain smiled and said, "I had to tell the general something! We're not going to the river crossing. We have business in town. I thought maybe you'd like to go see your old friend Mr. Dunnica. In the meantime, I plan to go see Ben Lewis at his home."

Josiah grinned, turned his horse, and rode off hollering over his shoulder, "See you at Boonville!"

Josiah knew precisely where W. F. Dunnica lived. His was one of the most beautiful houses in Glasgow. As president of the Glasgow Bank, he made a decent living before the war. However, being pro-Union, he made a fortune working hand in hand with the Union Provost Marshal, seizing the properties and assets of all Confederate sympathizers in the area. Since this was Sunday, very few people were out on Main Street. Josiah rode up to the house, dismounted, tied his horse to the front rail, and knocked on the door. Dunnica opened the front door to find two Navy Colt Revolvers in his face. "Mr. Dunnica! How nice to see you again. The last time I saw you, you were foreclosing on my uncle's farm!"

The banker, eyes wide open, backed up and declared, "I know you! You're that damned Riffel kid. I heard you joined up with them guerrillas. Also heard you'd been killed down at Fayette."

Josiah smiled and answered, "Well, I guess you heard wrong. If you'd be so kind as to get your coat, you and I are going to take a little walk down to the bank." W. F. Dunnica replied, "I most certainly will not."

Josiah grabbed him by the scruff of the neck and slammed him against the wall saying, "We can do this one of two ways. You can grab your coat, walk down to the bank, and let me in to make a withdrawal, or I can shoot you right here, take your keys, and go do it myself." He then cocked the hammer back on his pistol and stuck it under the banker's chin.

A few minutes later, Josiah and his newfound friend were unlocking the front door to the bank. After opening the vault, Josiah bound and gagged Dunnica in his office and proceeded to fill his saddlebags with the $21,000 that was stored in the safe. Bidding the banker a fond farewell, Josiah tipped his hat, walked out the front door of the bank, and rode off to Boonville.

While all this was going on, Bloody Bill and Little Archie arrived at the home of Benjamin Lewis, the wealthiest man in Glasgow. Their approach was a little different than that of Josiah. Dismounting their horses, Bill knocked on the front door, and when Mr. Lewis answered, Archie pistol-whipped him. Mr. Lewis staggered back into the living room, and Archie threw him into a chair and bound his hands and feet. Mr. Lewis, dazed from the blow to his head, looked up and said, "I know who you two are. You're Bloody Bill Anderson and Little Archie Clement. When people find out what you've done to me, there will be no place for you to hide."

Bill just laughed, "That's pretty bold talk for a pipsqueak banker tied to a chair in his own parlor." Lewis glared at Bloody Bill and stated, "You have no idea how much influence I have in this state."

Anderson laughed again and countered, "I couldn't care less how much influence you have. You, sir, picked the wrong side, and now you will pay."

Bill simply nodded at Archie who proceeded to beat Mr. Lewis to within an inch of his life. After 10 minutes, Bill shouted, "Don't kill him, Archie, he still needs to tell us the combination to that safe in his office. What do you think there, Mr. Lewis? You ready to give us the combination, or should I just let Archie beat you a while longer? He hasn't even used his knife — yet. He loves that part."

Lewis, who could barely see and was bleeding profusely, muttered the combination as he looked into the cold, steely eyes of Archie Clement. Bill went to the safe and removed $5,000 in gold and another $2,000 in bank notes. He walked back into the parlor and told Archie, "We got what we came for, let's go."

Archie, disappointed, looked at Bill and asked, "Can't I finish him? I've never had a banker's head before."

Bill smiled at Archie and said, "Maybe next time, my friend, but I want to see just how much influence Mr. Lewis here really has. Should be fun." With that, Bloody Bill tipped his hat to Mr. Lewis, and he and Archie headed out the door bound for Boonville.

SEPTEMBER 14, 1864, WEDNESDAY, CARSON CITY (DIARY)

"We have been traveling along the Carson River for the past four days. Arrived here in Carson City this afternoon. This is quite a pretty place in a valley and much larger than I expected. It was so cold this morning but has been very warm and dusty this afternoon. There was ice in the buckets when we awoke this morning. Lizzie and I walked around the town a little to see the place. I have got no letters here. We plan on staying here in town a few days before we set out to cross the mountains."

September 17, 1864, Lake Bigler (Diary)

"Left Carson City this morning and traveled over the Sierra Nevadas for the first time. They are beautiful. I never saw such grand pines in all my life and so many of them. Camped here in sight of beautiful, beautiful, Lake Bigler [Lake Tahoe]. I have heard of the beauties of this lake but I cannot describe them. My powers are too inferior to do the subject justice. It is the most beautiful site [sight] my eyes ever beheld. Lizzie and I walked down to the shore today and I gazed into its clear depths with the profoundest admiration. The thousands of little pebbles shine like diamonds in its bottom and it is surrounded with grand old pines trees."

"Have you ever seen anything as beautiful as this, Lizzie?" Matt asked as they stood on the shore of the lake.

"Why is it called Lake Bigler?" Lizzie wondered.

"Well, that is an interesting story," replied Matt. "Lieutenant John C. Fremont was here on a military expedition back in 1844. He explored most of this Western territory and became known as 'The Great Pathfinder.' *'The Prairie Finder,'* that book we used to prepare for this trip, was written based on the journal he kept during his travels and helped to lay out the Oregon Trail. He was the first white person to see this lake. Another explorer, John C. Johnson, who established the Johnson Cutoff Road we just traveled, came here several years later and named the lake, 'Lake Bigler,' in honor of California's third governor, John Bigler. Governor Bigler is a good Rebel just like us, and it seems the Union didn't like the fact that the lake was named after him. So, two years ago, the federal government changed the name of the lake to 'Lake Tahoe,' which is a Washoe Indian name that means 'Lake of the Sky.' So, if you're a Rebel, the lake is called Lake Bigler. If you're a Yankee, I guess you can call it Lake Tahoe. As for me, it is and always will be Lake Bigler. We best be getting back to camp before it gets dark."

OCTOBER 1864, 4 MILES SOUTH OF ALBANY, MISSOURI, RAY COUNTY

Having regrouped, Bill and his men sat around the campfire. "Boys," he said, "I just got word that General Price's forces were surrounded by Union troops who came in from Jefferson City, Sedalia, and Kansas City. Price managed to break through the Union lines to the south, but they were left with no choice but to retreat back to Arkansas. That pretty well leaves us to fend for ourselves from here on out."

As Bloody Bill was talking to his men, he was unaware that a local woman on a nearby farm saw him and his men ride by her place that afternoon and make camp down by the creek. She immediately rode into town to notify the local Provost Marshall. Majors Samuel P. Cox and John Grimes, along with 150 men of the 51st and 33rd Union infantry, prepared to ambush Bloody Bill and his men at first light.

Early the next morning, the Union forces arrived at a spot two miles east of the guerrilla camp. Major Cox signaled his troops to a halt and then turned in his saddle to Major Grimes and said, "This looks like as good a spot as any. I plan to give these damned Rebels a dose of their own medicine. There's plenty of cover on either side of the road in those trees. I want you to divide your men on either side of the road. Hold your fire until after the Rebels have passed your position. I will set my men up ahead at the bend in the road where we will stop their advance. As soon as you hear us open fire, you and your men need to sweep in behind them, and we will have them in a crossfire."

Major Grimes smiled and replied, "I've been wanting to do this since the first time these outlaws attacked my wagon train back in '63 using these same tactics. I kept trying to tell headquarters that we needed to adapt our way of fighting to match those of the guerrillas if we wanted to defeat them." Grimes continued to rant, "However, all those West Point graduates think they know everything about battle tactics, but there isn't anything in their books that explains how to fight an enemy who has no rules and has never read the book. I'll get my men in position and await your signal." He saluted, turned his horse, and started barking orders at his sergeant.

Before long, Anderson, Josiah, and a force of 50 guerrillas rode around the bend in the road and right into the trap. Bloody Bill stopped his horse. Josiah looked at him and asked, "What's wrong Bill?"

Anderson, still looking down the road, replied, "If I was going to set up an ambush, this is where I would do it. Something just doesn't look right." With that, he drew his pistols and charged forward. Major Grime's men, seeing Bill charging down the road, lost their patience and opened fire. Miraculously, Bill rode through the hail of bullets untouched. Josiah and the rest of the men, seeing there was no escape, charged forward behind their leader with guns blazing. Major Grimes and his men cut loose from the woods at point-blank range. When the smoke cleared, the road was filled with dead guerrillas, but Bloody Bill continued to charge forward until he ran right into Major Cox and his force of 100 men blocking the path.

Bill did not hesitate, and when he reached the Union line, his horse leaped over the blockade and continued on. Bill smiled at about the same time two Union Minie balls slammed into the back of his head. He threw his arms into the air and fell backward off his horse onto the dusty road where he drew his final breath. Bloody Bill died the way he always wanted to -- guns blazing while leading his men into battle.

When the shooting started from the woods on either side of the road, Josiah quickly summed up the situation and led his men to charge into the woods where the Union infantry dismounted. There, in a familiar environment, the guerrillas were able to quickly dispatch the riflemen who just killed so many of their friends. Josiah rode back up to the road just in time to see Bloody Bill and his horse clear the barricade, only to be shot down just a few yards farther. Little Archie Clement rode up to Josiah and yelled, "We have to go help him!" But Archie knew it was too late.

Josiah turned to him and replied, "Archie, you and I both know he's dead and that he went out the way he wanted to. I also know that he would want us to get the hell out of here and carry on with his work. Gather the rest of the men and let's git."

Archie turned in his saddle to have one final look down the road at his best friend lying dead before turning his horse and gathering the men.

After the battle, Major Cox gave the order to put Anderson's body in a wagon, and they transported him to nearby Richmond, Missouri. They dragged his body out of the wagon and sat it in a rocking chair on public display in front of the courthouse. People and reporters came from all around to see for themselves that Bloody Bill Anderson was undeniably dead and to have their photographs taken with the corpse. After two days of this, Bloody Bill was buried in an unmarked grave in the Richmond Cemetery.

The newspapers noted that, indeed, his horse's bridle was made of human scalps, and he was carrying six fully loaded revolvers when he was shot. Major Cox and Major Grimes became military heroes as a result of Anderson's death, and both received promotions. When word reached St. Louis headquarters that Anderson was dead, General Rosecrans directed that Anderson's watch and pistols be kept by the officers and that all the money found on the guerrillas be divided among the men.

OCTOBER 1864, EL DORADO, CALIFORNIA (DIARY)

"*We have made a good days travel came through Placerville. It is built in the Canyon of the Sierra Nevadas. Camped within 18 miles of Sacramento tonight and can it be that I am so near the place of our destination. It has been so very warm traveling. The country is very pretty here. Some prairie, but beautiful oaks scattered around in some places. Our camp tonight is under one of these huge oaks.*"

As they sat around the campfire that night, Sarah expressed her puzzlement: "Will, I'm confused. Some people have been calling this place Hangtown, others call it Placerville. Which one is it?"

Will leaned back, took a swig from a jug of whiskey, and then responded, "Placerville was a "gold rush" town named after the placer gold deposits found in the nearby riverbeds and hills in the late 1840s. The town sits halfway between Sacramento and Lake Bigler (Tahoe)."

He took another swig and continued. "The gold was first discovered in 1848, just 10 miles from here at Sutter's Mill. That triggered the California Gold Rush of '49 which brought thousands of prospectors to California. During the gold rush, Placerville boomed as an essential supply center for the surrounding mining camps."

"I see. That explains Placerville," said Sarah. "But what about Hangtown?"

Will took another belt of whiskey and explained, "Placerville was also known as Hangtown in its early days. The most famous story of how the town got its name was something that happened back before the gold rush. A gambler named Lopez won big at poker one night at the local saloon. After he went to bed that evening, several outlaws came to his room and tried to rob him. Lopez fought back, and hearing the commotion, several other people from the town helped him capture the would-be robbers. With no evidence, the mob accused the thieves of being wanted elsewhere for murder and robbery."

"With no more evidence than that," Will resumed, "the people held a 30-minute trial on the spot, and a unanimous guilty verdict was given. The crowd demanded the men be sentenced to death by hanging, and the sentence was immediately carried out. So, until the gold rush days, Placerville was known as Hangtown. That ought to be enough stories for the night. We need to turn in. We have a big day tomorrow!"

JAMES WAKEFIELD FARM, SPENCER COUNTY, KENTUCKY

Quantrill, hearing the news of General Price's retreat and Bloody Bill's death, could see the writing on the wall. The war would soon be over. He headed south out of Missouri with 30 of his men and arrived at the farm of James Wakefield in Spencer County, Kentucky. A wanted man, Quantrill changed his name to Captain Clarke, and he and his men conducted raids on the local Union militia.

Camped out in the barn lot, Lieutenant George Todd, Quantrill's second-in-command asked, "Do you have a plan of where we go from here?"

Quantrill replied, "No, son, I don't. I just know that if we had stayed in Missouri, we eventually would have been caught and hanged. At least here in Kentucky, we are surrounded by good Southerners, and when the war comes to an end, we will stand a much better chance of surviving when we turn ourselves in."

About that time, a rifle shot rang out. It was immediately followed by a barrage of bullets. A Union Ranger force under Captain Edward Terrill, who was given the assignment to hunt down the guerrillas, surrounded the barn lot and snuck up on the unsuspecting guerrillas, setting up the perfect ambush. As several of Quantrill's men fell dead, the captain jumped up and ran for his horse but was shot in the back and fell to the ground paralyzed from the waist down.

When the shooting stopped, Captain Terrill walked up to the wounded Quantrill and said, "Captain, we've been looking for you for over a month. We know who you are, and you have been our number one priority ever since you arrived in Kentucky. Back in Missouri, they would've killed you right here, but the Union doesn't operate that way here in Kentucky. You are now a prisoner of war and will be afforded all the rights of a military prisoner. My job was to capture you, which I have done. I will leave it up to the courts to decide what your fate will be. Our medic will treat you here, and as soon as he has you stabilized, you will be taken to the hospital at the military prison in Louisville." Those were the last words Quantrill heard before he passed out. The medic tended to the captain's wound, and he was loaded into a wagon and taken to the prison hospital.

Two days later, Quantrill awoke in a hospital ward at the prison. The pain he was experiencing was unbelievable, and he screamed as soon as he became conscious. A doctor approached his bedside, "Captain, you have been put in my charge. I am Dr. Johnson, and I've been treating you for the past two days. I'm going to be straight with you. The wound you received has lodged a bullet next to your spine, and you are paralyzed from the waist down. I will give you morphine for the pain, but I can do nothing more until a decision is made to operate and remove the bullet. Unfortunately, this is not my decision. A military tribunal is being held as we speak. Some of the members would just as soon that I leave you here to suffer in pain and eventually die. Others think you have valuable information that could help us round up the last of the guerrillas in Missouri, and they are in favor of proceeding with the operation in the hopes that we can save your life, so you can testify in a military court." The doctor gave Quantrill a dose of morphine, and Quantrill's vision slowly faded to black.

Sometime later, Bill Quantrill again awoke. The pain was excruciating, and the doctor administered another dose of morphine saying, "Captain, I cut this dose in half. You can't heal if you're out cold all the time."

Shortly after, a Catholic priest approached. He pulled up a chair next to the bed and stated, "Son, I'm Father O'Toole. I'm the chaplain here at the prison. I want you to know that I don't care if you are Union or Confederate. I also don't care about your past. In my eyes, we are all God's children, and I am here to help and comfort you."

Quantrill turned to the priest and replied, "Father, I was born and raised in the Presbyterian Church and attended services every Sunday until I left home at the age of 16. I have to admit, I've lost my way, but lying here on my deathbed, I feel it is time to make amends with my creator."

Father O'Toole smiled and gently placed his hand on Quantrill's forehead. "Fear not, my son. I will be here by your side and prepare you for your final journey."

While in the hospital, Quantrill met with the priest every day for two weeks, made a full confession of his sins, and was baptized into the Roman Catholic faith. Several days later, the decision was handed down from the military tribunal to proceed with the surgery. Unfortunately, Quantrill died on the operating table and was buried in the Catholic cemetery in Louisville.

SEPTEMBER 23, 1864, SACRAMENTO CALIFORNIA (DIARY)

"*Our journey is at last completed and we are here safe in Sacramento. It is a beautiful place with so many shade trees and beautiful flowers. I don't know yet how I shall like the place.*"

In 1839, John Sutter and his friends arrived in California and built Fort Sutter on the American River just upstream from where it joins the Sacramento River. Soon, other businessmen arrived in the area looking for opportunities. When gold was discovered in the nearby foothills in 1848, the small commercial center, then known as Sutter's Embarcadero, was flooded with prospectors and soon became known as the City of Sacramento. It rapidly became the main trading center for the miners outfitting themselves for the gold fields.

Sacramento's waterfront location was great for transporting goods but was known for severe flooding. The city also had numerous fires because its buildings were nothing more than temporary wood and canvas structures. The area was wiped out by floods in 1850, 1852, and again in 1862. Something had to be done.

After supper, Matt and Lizzie took take a walk to check out the city. They were amazed by the number of people, new construction, and wagons passing to and fro. Lizzie asked Matt, "Do you think it is always this busy around here?"

Matt, jumping out of the way of two men carrying lumber down the boardwalk answered, "Well, yes and no. They say the town is growing by leaps and bounds and has been ever since the gold rush started. But I also heard that this place has been wiped out by floods at least three times, and the decision has been made to haul in tons of dirt to raise the main street above the flood stage. If you notice, half of those wagons are filled with dirt. As soon as they finish raising a section of the street, businesses are coming in behind them and building new buildings that will no longer flood every time the river comes up. Over there is the new bank building, and there is a new hotel and saloon that just opened on the corner. The work going on across the street is for a new general store."

Lizzie smiled and asserted, "So, just like us, the town is new here as well! How exciting!"

"I never thought of it that way, but you are right," Matt replied. "Let's see if we can find the school where I will teach."

Just two blocks away, the girls came upon the schoolhouse. It was a simple structure that housed a total of four small classrooms. The steep roof was topped with a bell tower used for calling the children to class and signaling the end of the school day. As they approached, they were met by a tall, thin gentleman sporting a tweed suit complete with matching vest. "May I help you, ladies? I am headmaster John Keeney here at the Sacramento Elementary Academy."

Matt smiled and replied, "Hello, Mr. Keeney. I am Mattie Logan, and this is my cousin, Lizzie! It is such a pleasure to meet you in person finally. I hope you received my latest letters."

Mr. Keeney approached Mattie, extended his hand, and with a broad smile, exclaimed, "Of course, I did! I am so excited to meet you and have you join our school as a teacher. I have reviewed your qualifications and have corresponded with your former headmaster back in Littleby. He had nothing but the highest praise for you! When can you start?"

Matt grabbed Mr. Keeney's hand and shook it vigorously, answering, "We just arrived today. We haven't even found a permanent place to stay yet and are camped just on the outskirts of town. I should be settled in and ready to start by the end of next week if that is acceptable."

"Absolutely," Mr. Keeney replied. "If there is anything I or any of the other teachers can do to help get you settled, please, let us know."

Mattie looked up at the bell tower and replied, "Just let me ring the classes to session week after next. I'm ecstatic. See you then!"

Mr. Keeney said, "Excellent! Until then."

SPRING 1865, GUERILLA CAMP, 4 MILES SE OF LEXINGTON, MISSOURI

Josiah and little Archie awoke early, and as they sat by the small campfire drinking their morning coffee, Josiah said to Clement, "I love springtime in Missouri. It is hard to believe that such a beautiful place could be the home of so many terrible events. Everything is so green, and the dogwoods are blooming, bringing new life to this troubled land. Archie, maybe it is time for us to start a new life as well. The papers say that General Lee has surrendered to General Grant at some place called Appomattox Courthouse. I've also heard that General Joe Johnston surrendered in North Carolina. It is only a matter of time before General Kirby Smith surrenders the Army of the Trans-Mississippi to the Yankees. Let's face it; the war is over, and we've lost."

Archie glared at Josiah with his steely blue eyes and replied, "You do whatever you want. I do not believe a word the paper says. I will continue the fight until the day I die. I probably am the most wanted man in Missouri right now, and if I am captured, there will be no trial. I will surely be hanged, but I will not go down without a fight." Archie reached over to pick up a newspaper and said, "Let me read you something, Josiah. This is on the front page of the *Columbia Statesman*."

"Let the sight of a guerrilla be the signal to shoot him. If he comes to your house, shoot him. If you see him on the road, shoot him down. In short, resolve that those devils shall no longer rob, insult, and outrage you, and hold in jeopardy your property and very existence."

Archie tossed the paper aside and asked, "Josiah, do really think after hearing that, I could get a fair trial?"

Seeing the rage in Archie's eyes, Josiah responded, "Martial law has now ended here in Missouri. People are tired of this war, Archie. Union Colonel Harding has been chasing us down for months now. All the Central District Militia Cavalry are out there looking for us as we speak. Several of our boys went into town yesterday, and their contacts told them that if they surrendered, the Union commander in Lexington would treat them as prisoners of war, not guerrillas. They said his name is Major Davis. Several of us talked last night, and we are going to send a message to the major to ask for terms. I am tired of fighting, Archie. I just want to go home, find Mattie, and live a normal life. If you want to send a message to Major Davis asking for your own separate terms, I understand. But as for me and most of the boys here, we are done."

Archie grimaced and replied, "I don't blame you, Josiah, you have something to go home to. I do not. It has been one helluva run, and I will always consider you my friend. We should split up today so that you are not associated with me and the boys who choose to continue the fight. Good luck, my friend." The two men stood and shook hands. Archie turned and shouted orders to break camp.

Josiah gathered together all the men who made the decision to surrender. He chose one of their ranks to ride into town and inform Colonel Harding that Josiah and his men were willing to turn themselves in, provided they could ride into town unharmed, lay down their arms, sign an oath of loyalty to the Union, and go home to live in peace. About 11 a.m., the rider returned with word that the terms were acceptable.

At noon, Josiah sent a rider into town carrying a white flag. A squad of soldiers rode out to escort Josiah and the guerrillas to Lexington. One man rode right up to Josiah, saluted, and said, "Sir, I am Colonel Harding."

Josiah returned the salute and replied, "I am Josiah Riffel. I have here with me 85 men of the Confederacy. We wish to surrender based on the terms we sent you."

Harding smiled and said, "Relax, Josiah. We wish you no harm. We all want to see this conflict end as well so we can get home to our families. The men I brought with me are here to protect you, not harm you. Follow us." With that, he turned his horse and led the procession back to town.

They rode straight to the Provost Marshal's office on Main Street, and at Josiah's command, dismounted in unison, stepped two paces forward, and laid down their weapons. Each man filed before the Provost Marshal where he raised his right hand and took an oath of allegiance to the United States. Each of the former guerrillas received the parole certificate. They returned to their horses and were told by Colonel Harding to return home and live in peace.

Word quickly spread through the local papers of the guerrillas' surrender, and Josiah became something of a celebrity with the Union command for having negotiated the surrender. The following week, Josiah was approached by Colonel Harding, who praised him for negotiating the terms of the surrender, and asked if he would be interested in working as a liaison between the Union command and the remaining guerrillas in the field to get them to surrender as he and his men did. Josiah agreed to take the job, not because he supported the Union, but merely to end the bloodshed once and for all.

10 miles south of the City of Lexington, Lafayette County, Missouri

Since Bloody Bill was dead, and Josiah and the bulk of the boys turned themselves in, Archie found himself with only a handful of men. Even though there was a price on his head, most people, with the war over, didn't seem interested in collecting the bounty. Archie spent the majority of his time visiting old friends in the area. When the war came to an end, the Missouri State Government passed a new law requiring all men 18 and older to register for possible drafting into the Missouri State Militia. The state did not want a repeat of what happened at the outset of the Civil War and sought to assure that they could form a militia at a moment's notice, should trouble arise in the future.

Archie and his few men saw this and thought it would be hilarious if they were to ride into Lexington and register for the draft. So, Archie sent word to the Provost Marshal in Lexington that he was coming into town to register, and he would not cause trouble if the Union forces left them alone. The next day, word was returned to Archie and his men that they could come into town, and the Union soldiers would not bother them.

Archie and his men, a force of 25, rode into Lexington the following morning. The first place they stopped was the city hotel and headed straight for the saloon. After they drank their fill and had lunch, they headed to the courthouse where each of them registered for the draft and were told it would be best if they left town. They complied, but about an hour later, Archie rode into town alone and returned to the saloon.

Word reached Union Major Bacon Montgomery, commander of the State Militia at Lexington, that Archie rode back into town alone and was at the local saloon. Major Montgomery immediately sent three of his men to the saloon to arrest Archie. When the soldiers stepped into the bar, Archie pulled his pistols and killed all three. He then bolted out the door, hopped on his horse, and galloped up Franklin Street. As he did, every window on Franklin Street opened where rifles protruded. Almost in unison, the citizens of Lexington opened fire. Archie was hit numerous times and fell dead from his horse in the middle of the street, ending his reign of terror.

GUERRILLA CAMP 5 MILES EAST OF ROCHEPORT, MISSOURI

As Josiah neared the camp, he heard the shrill whistle of one of the pickets signaling the guerrillas that a rider was approaching. This was the eighth such camp Josiah visited over the past two months. In every case, after he discussed the terms, the guerrillas accepted his offer to lead them to the local Provost Marshal, lay down their arms, take an oath of loyalty to the Union, and go home to their families. He thought this time would be no different.

When he came within sight of the camp, a single shot rang out, and he fell from his horse. As he lay on the ground, four guerrillas stepped out of the brush. A tall, scruffy-looking guerrilla with long black hair and a graying beard approached him. "We know who you are, Josiah, and we've been waiting for you, the man said. Although the South has surrendered, in this state, the war will never end until the last of us is killed by those Union devils who invaded our state, killed our families, and took everything we had. I know you think you have been doing the right thing getting our folks to surrender, and you've been damn good at it. But we could not allow you to continue to reduce our numbers while we carry on the fight. You were always a great Rebel, but you have simply lost your way." He turned and gave his men the order to mount up. As Josiah's vision began to fade, the last thing he saw was the leader of the guerrillas look back, salute him, and ride off.

Josiah slowly opened his eyes. The pain in his gut immediately struck him. *Where am I? What happened?* Lying there, he slowly began to remember his encounter with the guerrillas. He remembered falling from his horse and the evil look in the eyes of the man who shot him. After that, nothing. As his eyes began to focus, Josiah looked around the room. The small candle in the corner of the room provided the only light. It appeared he was in some sort of cellar. The walls were made of stone. He was lying on the floor and was covered with a down comforter. An old man sitting on a wooden chair rose and slowly approached him. He kneeled next to Josiah, pulled the cover back and checked his wound. "Hi there," he said. "I'm Doc Haggerty. I've been worried about you, son. When they brought you in here, I honestly didn't think you'd make it. I did the best I could to patch you up. You took a round just above your hip. Lucky for you, the bullet passed straight through and didn't hit any bone. My greatest concern was an infection, but I cleaned and dressed your wound as soon as they brought you here. You've been in and out of it for five days. How do you feel?"

"I feel like I've been kicked by a mule," replied Josiah. "Where are we and how did I get here?"

"Well, they tell me a Union patrol found an abandoned guerrilla camp, and you were laying face down at the edge of the clearing. They figured you were dead, but when one of the soldiers was searching you for papers, he noticed you were still breathing. The captain of the patrol figured you were a guerrilla, and if you survived, they could get valuable information as to where your buddies are hiding out. So, they loaded you up and brought you here to St. Louis. You are in the Gratiot Street Prison for Confederate prisoners. You're damn lucky they brought you here. Before the war, this building was a medical college. It was owned by Dr. Joseph McDowell. The good doctor was a strong Southern sympathizer, and when the war started, he took his medical skills and joined the Confederacy, currently serving as a doctor in General Lee's army. In the fall of '61, the Union Army seized this place and turned it into a prison for all the Southern sympathizers being captured in Missouri. The prison is a big place, and we are right in the middle of St. Louis. A few rules. This place has a courtyard, but it is minimal. They let us out for fresh air twice a day. Because the courtyard is so small, and there are so many of us here, we spill out onto the street in front of the building when we are let out there. The good news is, it allows us to make contact with the local population. The bad news is, the guards have orders to shoot to kill anyone who tries to wander off. Several of the prisoners have been successful in mingling with the crowds on the street and escaping. But many more have been gunned down trying that trick. The biggest concern we have here is the overcrowding. This place was supposed to hold 500 prisoners. Right now, we have 1,100 men and women being held here. The sanitary conditions and the lack of food have taken a much higher toll than the guards with their rifles. That is why I was so concerned about you getting an infection. It is sad to say, but the mortality rate in this prison is 50 percent."

"Well, Doc," Josiah replied, "I don't plan on being part of that 50 percent, and I sure as hell don't plan on staying here. You see, I was a guerrilla, and I guess I still am, but when I was shot, I was working for Union Colonel Harding. I could see the war was coming to an end, and I just want the bloodshed to be over. So, I was asked by Colonel Harding to go out and contact the remaining guerrillas in the state and negotiate terms for them to surrender and go home to live in peace. Obviously, not all the guerrillas are willing to give up the fight," Josiah explained pointing at his wound. "That is how I wound up here."

Doc stared at Josiah for a minute and said, "That's a really good story, but I doubt the warden or any of the guards here are going to believe you. Right now, you just need to concentrate on getting better."

SACRAMENTO ELEMENTARY ACADEMY, SACRAMENTO CALIFORNIA.

Having worked at the school for nearly 4 months, Mattie was settled into a routine with her students. She absolutely loved the job, and the children loved her. It was a happy place in which Matt could take her mind off all her past troubles and her endless grief over whether her true love, Josiah, survived the conflict back home. Just the day before, she received a note from home. In it, her father broke the news to her that Josiah and his men surrendered in Lexington, but Josiah was continuing to work with the Union to convince the guerrillas to capitulate. He went on to say that Josiah brought in seven groups of guerrillas but went into the field three weeks ago, and no one heard from him since. He wrote that the Union Command feared that he was killed by the guerrillas for aiding them. Matt was devastated by the letter but refused to give up hope, and she wrote back to her father telling him so. After a long hard cry, she cleaned up and headed off to school.

GRATIOT STREET PRISON, ST. LOUIS, MISSOURI

Six months passed, and aside from a slight limp, Josiah recovered from his wound. Just as Doc Haggerty said, when Josiah was questioned by his captors, they didn't believe a word. He pleaded with them to contact Colonel Harding and verify his story. The warden refused, telling him that every prisoner being held at Gratiot Street claimed they were innocent.

Lexington, Missouri, Office of the Provost Marshall

Union Colonel Harding, the Provost Marshal, called out from his desk. "Captain, please come in here."

The captain entered the room, came to attention, and saluted. "Yes, sir?"

"Captain, how are we coming with our efforts to bring the remaining guerrilla bands before us and surrender?" Colonel Harding inquired.

The Captain replied, "Sir, I think we've cleaned out most of them, but I have to admit, without the help of that kid, Josiah Riffel, we have no way of knowing where or how many guerrillas are still out there." Colonel Harding sat there for a moment before responding.

"Captain, I have often wondered what happened to that young man. I find it hard to believe that he would rejoin those outlaws. However, I can't imagine what else could have happened. Surely, if he were dead, we would've heard something from the locals."

"I agree, sir, but he has also not shown up in any of the remaining activities of the guerrillas locally. Maybe he fled south to Mexico with the rest of those Southern cowards," replied the captain.

"No, I don't think so. We know he was seeing that Logan girl from up at Littleby. I have made inquiries of her father who is now living in Mexico, Missouri, with his family. He claims he has heard nothing from Josiah and has informed his daughter that the boy is probably dead. Old man Logan lost everything during the war, and his farm was sold on the courthouse steps. He hates the Union. If Josiah were still fighting for the guerrillas, he would have told us so. I just can't figure it out. Any thoughts?"

"Well, sir, if he isn't fighting for the guerrillas and he's not dead, there is only one other possibility."

"And what might that be?" inquired the Colonel.

"Perhaps he was taken prisoner. There are literally thousands of people locked up in jails and prisons throughout the state. Quite frankly, the system is broken. As the war progressed, we simply were not equipped to imprison that many folks. So, when the local jails overfilled, we decided to start construction of the federal prison in Alton, Illinois. When Josiah went missing, the local jails were full, and the Alton Prison was still under construction at that time, so we told the Provost Marshals statewide to ship their prisoners to St. Louis where we seized some buildings and created two temporary prisons. One was an old slave market, the Myrtle Street Prison, and the other was a Medical College, the Gratiot Street Prison. If, by chance, Josiah was picked up by a random patrol and taken prisoner, the first place I would look would be St. Louis."

"Make it so, captain, and let me know what you find out. If that poor boy is rotting in prison, with what he has done to help us, he deserves his freedom."

Gratiot Street Prison, St. Louis, Missouri

Josiah shielded his eyes from the bright sunlight as he stepped through the gates of the prison and out onto the street. He found it hard to believe that he survived his imprisonment and was now free. It came as a shock when the warden called him to his office and informed him that Colonel Harding contacted the warden and verified Josiah's story. The warden offered no apology, and in Josiah's mind, none was required. The warden, like all soldiers during the war, was only doing his job. Josiah stood on the street for a long time contemplating his next move. He only had the clothes on his back and no money.

"Josiah! Josiah!" he heard someone shouting from across the street. He couldn't believe his eyes. It was his old friend Doug Sharp. He and Doug fought together under General Price in the Missouri State Guard at the start of the war. Doug ran up to Josiah and threw his arms around him. "Josiah, what are you doing here? I haven't seen you in three years."

Josiah, still in shock at seeing his friend, replied, "I was just released from prison.

Doug intently looked at his friend, "You were in there? I had no idea."

Josiah smiled and replied, "Evidently you are not the only one!"

"Well, Josiah, you look like hell, and I aim to fix that. I live just down the street. Let's get you some proper clothes and a decent meal. Then we can talk."

After taking a long, hot bath and donning a pair of canvas pants and a soft cotton shirt, Josiah slipped on the socks and the boots that his friend Doug gave him. He stepped into the small parlor and saw that Doug and his wife Tonya were already seated at the table with mountains of food before them.

Tonya jumped up and gave Josiah a hug. "Doug has filled me in on your story. Do you have any idea what you will do now?"

Josiah sat down at the table, and although he was starving, he took the time to answer her question before digging in. I must find Matt. Last I heard, she was nearly to California. I pray to God she made it there safely. I have no idea where to look in California, so, my first stop will be in Littleby to visit the Logan family farm. Hopefully, her parents can give me some answers. My problem is, I have no money and no way to get there."

Doug told Josiah, "You, sir, will be provided everything you need to get to Littleby and on to California. You saved my life at Wilson's Creek, and I will never forget it. I came home to St. Louis after I was wounded and set up a very successful shipping business. I started with only two small boats ferrying goods across the river. The Union probably knew my background but was willing to look the other way because of my riverboat skills. From there, I built up a fleet of paddle wheelers and made a fortune transporting goods and people up and down the Mississippi. Tomorrow morning, I will book you a seat on the train to Littleby. I will also bankroll you with enough funds to travel by stage as far west as you can get and then purchase a horse and gear to travel the remainder of your journey."

Josiah looked on in disbelief. "Doug, I cannot accept such a generous offer."

Tonya interjected, "Josiah, Doug told me how you ran out under fire and pulled him to safety there on Bloody Hill during the battle. If not for you, we would have none of what we have today, and I would not have my husband. You will take our offer; this discussion is over. Let's eat."

Josiah thought long and hard about Doug and Tanya's offer and realized he had no choice. If he ever wanted to see Matt again, he had to accept. The next morning, Josiah boarded the train for Littleby. As he traveled through the countryside, he observed the devastation. What once stood as beautiful homes were now nothing more than a stone chimney surrounded by ashes. Crops lay fallow in the fields overrun by weeds. As the train stopped at small towns along the way, people gathered, and he saw the hopeless desperation in their eyes. Many had lost everything including their loved ones. Josiah thought: "*This is the part of war no one sees. Politicians and generals sit behind their desks and make decisions that devastate the lives of so many people.*" As the train pulled into Littleby, Josiah could not help but think of Matt sitting on the bench along the station wall waiting for her trip west. It was almost as if he could see her sitting there with tears in her eyes wondering if they would ever be together again.

LITTLEBY, MISSOURI, AUDRAIN COUNTY, LOGAN FAMILY FARM

It was a short hike from the train station to the Logan family farm. As Josiah approached the house, it looked the same, but several young children were playing near the barn. He wondered to himself, *"Have I been gone so long that Matt's sisters now have children? Surely not."* He stepped up onto the front porch and knocked on the door. A short, stocky man with a full beard answered the door. "Can I help you?" he asked.

"Who are you?" inquired the puzzled Josiah.

"I am Stuart Kraus, and this is my home. Who the hell are you?" he demanded with a thick German accent. Josiah was taken aback. Who was this little man now claiming to be the owner of the Logan family farm?

"I am Josiah Riffel, and I am here looking for the Logans; where are they?" Josiah asked.

"The Logans? Are you talking about the people that used to live here? They are gone. Damned southern sympathizers lost this place when the Provost Marshall found out they were supporting those murdering Rebel thugs. Provost seized this place and put it up for auction on the courthouse steps the next day. I bought it fair and square." It took all of Josiah's power to keep from choking the man to death right there, but he knew he needed to find out more information.

"Do you have any idea where they went?" asked Josiah.

"The Logan's? Last I heard most of the damned Rebels who lost their farms around here moved to Mexico, Missouri. Good place for them. Nothing there but a whistle-stop for the rail line." Josiah, realizing he would get nothing more from this man, turned, stepped down from the porch, and began walking back to the train station.

Mexico, Missouri, Audrain County

It was just a short hop from Littleby to Mexico, and as Josiah stepped off the train, he saw it was very similar to all the other stops he had seen along the way. As he walked into the station, he approached the stationmaster at the ticket booth and inquired, "Excuse me, sir, I am looking for some friends."

The stationmaster looked up and with a smile said, "These days we're all looking for friends. What can I do to help you?"

Josiah returned the smile and asked, "Do you by chance know the Logans?"

The man's smile grew larger and he answered, "Of course, I do. I've been seeing Mr. Logan's daughter, Anna."

Josiah couldn't believe his luck. He immediately exclaimed, "Can you take me there. I must see Mr. Logan!"

"Calm down there, fella; as soon as the train pulls out, I'm done for the day, and I'd be happy to take you to see him." Shortly after that, the train pulled away from the station, the ticketmaster closed up shop, and led Josiah down Main Street where they arrived at a small home with a broad front porch and a yard surrounded by a white picket fence. Sure enough, sitting on the front porch was Matt's father. He saw Josiah coming and immediately jumped up and ran into the yard to greet him. As Josiah reached Mr. Logan, he embraced Josiah and exclaimed, "My God, son, we all thought you were dead!" He then hollered back to the house, "Mother, girls, come quick! Look who's here!" Matt's mother and the girls all rushed to Josiah and embraced him. It was a miracle. They could not believe Josiah survived the war. That evening, as they all sat around the dinner table, they exchanged their stories of what transpired during the previous years. Matt's father pulled out the letters he received from Matt since she arrived in California, including her reply to the one he sent telling her that he feared Josiah was dead.

SACRAMENTO ELEMENTARY ACADEMY, SACRAMENTO, CALIFORNIA

"Children, turn to page 39 of your McGuffey's Reader," instructed Matt. "Your assignment last night was to read the story titled 'The Good-natured Boy.' Sally, would you like to summarize for the class what the story was about?"

A pretty, little, blonde girl with blue eyes, wearing a simple cotton dress, Sally stood next to her desk and replied, "Yes, Miss Logan. It was a wonderful story about a little boy named Henry who was walking to a friend's house five miles away. During his trip, he found a half-starved dog and gave him some of his food. A short time later, he came upon a horse lying down by the road, and the boy gave him food and water as well. Later, he came upon a blind man in a stream who was lost, and he helped him to shore, and finally that day, he met an old soldier on crutches who was hobbling down the road, and the boy gave him what was left of his food and water."

Matt stopped her there and continued, "William, would you like to tell us the rest of the story?"

William jumped up from his seat, smiled, and said, "Yes, Miss Logan." Matt instructed him to proceed." William, sitting in the front row, turned to the rest of the class and spoke: "The young boy spent his day helping others and found himself lost in the woods at night with no food. Shortly after he sat next to a tree, the dog he helped came up with a handkerchief in his mouth, and inside the handkerchief was some bread. Sitting with the dog, the horse approached, so the boy hopped on its back, and the horse took him back to the road. But then, two bad men appeared and tried to rob the boy and take his horse. About that time, the old crippled soldier and the blind man arrived and scared off the robbers."

Matt looked at the class and asked, "What did you learn from this story children?"

A small, dark-headed girl named Annie, seated in the back of the room, raised her hand and answered, "If you help other people, they will help you."

Matt smiled and replied, "That is exactly right. We should always help people regardless of who they are or where they came from." A young boy named Timmy, sporting a cotton shirt, work pants, and suspenders, raised his hand. "Yes, Timmy," said Matt, pointing to the boy.

Timmy stood next to his desk and asked, "Miss Logan, is the soldier in the story like your friend Josiah who you have told us about? He sounds like a brave and kind man like your friend."

Matt, fighting back the tears welling in her eyes, replied, "Yes, Timmy, he was ... is just like the soldier in the story." She caught herself in mid-sentence referring to Josiah in the past tense.

Unable to continue for fear she would break down in front of the children, she told them to turn to the next lesson and read the story to themselves. Turning to her desk at the front of the room, she sat down, bowed her head, and asked herself: *"How can I possibly go on today? My heart is broken. What will my future hold without Josiah? No one could ever replace him."* With her head still bowed and tears rolling down her cheeks, the door at the back of the room swung open, flooding the room with light. Matt quickly dried her eyes and stood. Standing in the doorway was the silhouette of a man back-lighted by the brilliant sunlight. Matt, thinking it was Mr. Keeney, said, "Good day, Principal Keeney. We were just going over our lesson from last night, and the children are now reading the next story in our book."

The figure stepped forward, and Matt noticed that it was not Mr. Keeney, but a tall man using a cane as he limped into the room. Wearing a broad-brimmed hat, the man lifted his head and said, "That's very good, Miss Logan, but do you suppose you could get a substitute for the rest of the day? I have traveled a long way to see you."

Matt couldn't believe her eyes! Standing before her was Josiah. She ran forward, threw her arms around him, and nearly knocked him over, while shouting, "Children, this is Josiah!" The children all cheered.

As Matt and Josiah embraced, Josiah looked into Matt's tearful eyes, smiled, and simply said, "Let's go home."

The End

Made in the USA
Coppell, TX
21 July 2022